THE COLUMNIST

---
*   *   *

JEFFREY FRANK

A NOVEL

SIMON & SCHUSTER

NEW YORK   LONDON   TORONTO   SYDNEY   SINGAPORE

SIMON & SCHUSTER
Rockefeller Center
1230 Avenue of the Americas
New York NY 10020

This book is a work of fiction. Names, characters,
places, and incidents either are products of the
author's imagination or are used fictitiously. Any
resemblance to actual events or locales or persons,
living or dead, is entirely coincidental.

SIMON & SCHUSTER and colophon are registered trademarks
of Simon & Schuster, Inc.

Book design by Ellen R. Sasahara

Manufactured in the United States of America

1   3   5   7   9   10   8   6   4   2

Library of Congress Cataloging-in-Publication Data
Frank, Jeffrey.
The Columnist: a novel/Jeffrey Frank.
p.   cm.
1. Journalists—Fiction. 2. Washington (D.C.)—Fiction. I. Title.
PS3556.R33423 C6   2001   813'.54—dc21   00-69818
ISBN 0-7432-1253-3

For Adam, my father;
for Thomas Adam, his grandson;
and, again, Diana

* * *

My father, as he lay dying, was astounded when I told him that I was writing a memoir, with its claims on the tradition of a *Bildungsroman*, and perhaps he was right to be skeptical. What is ordinarily wanted from someone like me are observations about consequential people, and certainly I have my impressions of famous men and women, and how it was to be quite near them for a time. I will get to that. But there are other matters that need explanation, wounds that still require stitches.

I'm in my study on a bright day in October at the end of the century. On my shelves are the mementos that one collects (photographs, prizes); I'm surrounded by books, most of them history and biography (the important David McCullough), along with a smattering of excellent fiction. I began to jot down my recollections after a conversation with George Bush the elder, at a cocktail party in the home of a wise Cabinet officer, one of those happy occasions when everything is "off the record," when we're Americans first and antagonists second.

"I've always thought that you tried to be fair, Brandon," Bush said, chuckling gamely. "Not that you weren't tough, but you always put your country first."

I nodded with gratitude and, as a white-jacketed black man passed us with a pewter tray, reached for a spinach quiche the size of a half-dollar. The former President looked lank and fit. As we spoke, I sensed that others close by were trying to overhear, perhaps in the hope of learning yet another detail about matters of which I've never spoken publicly. I disappointed them.

"You've had an interesting life," Bush continued. "I was talking about this only the other day with Bar, and we were saying that Brandon Sladder must know everyone who matters. We never missed your column. Of course, you guys in the media get the last word."

Now it was my turn to chuckle, for it is a commonly held view that we have that advantage.

"I've been lucky, Mr. President," I said, and saw that he was pleased at the honorific. Over the years, I've discovered that people enjoy hearing their titles: Mr. Ambassador, Senator, what-have-you.

"It's more than that," said Bush, and he gave me a warm look. "You've been there, Brandon. You were there when I met Mr. Gorbachev, but you were there when Kennedy sat in my favorite chair."

I knew Jack Kennedy, of course, and supposed that I had

a story or two to tell about him. But I knew Jack only slightly; he belonged to another era—to men like Joe Alsop and Scotty Reston. I quickly corrected the former President on that score.

"You still ought to write it down, Brandon," Bush continued and he patted me softly on my right shoulder, letting his fingers linger there for an extra, affectionate second. "Don't hold back," he added.

A few minutes later, I spoke to our host. We'd known each other for years, and he looked at me with enormous sympathy as he told me about an important policy change toward another of those hostile little nations that remind one of poisonous insects. By this time, though, my thoughts were elsewhere—on my next column, of course (I permitted myself a quick, private *tour d'horizon*), and what I'd say on my television appearance that very evening. As I drove to the studio, I found myself haunted by the former President's suggestion that I could add considerably more than a footnote to a chronicle of our time.

*　　*　　*

In the spirit of a *Bildungsroman*, I may as well begin in the fall of 1957, when I was eighteen and enrolled at Darleigh College (founded in 1799 in the leafy village of Old Drake, Massachusetts). Even as a young man, I was frustrated at the smallness of my surroundings and a shortage of serious people. Compared to Buffalo, my birthplace, Old Drake was a backwater.

I got off to a particularly bad start in my freshman year, when it was my misfortune to get a roommate whose personal habits were cloddish. The large and hairy George Kipler III—his few friends called him "Kip"—refused for weeks to bathe, or spray, and had a habit of cackling suddenly and announcing that he'd "cut the cheese." That was bad enough, and I pleaded with him to reform; but as that first year progressed, Kip flouted the rules and began to bring

his girlfriend into our small quarters. Soon enough, they became unbearable. His friend, who had an unforgettable red
pimple on her buttocks and asymmetrical breasts, paraded
about, although I tried not to notice, and the two of them
made it clear, as they ground together beneath his spotted
pink blanket, that they wanted to be alone. I warned them
several times that my studies came first; and when I reluctantly acted in my own best interest and reported their behavior, the consequences were severe. Kip and his friend
were suspended, and decided to transfer to more permissive
schools. Of course, I paid a severe price, too; Kip urinated
on my clothing, and many Darleigh students, who heard
about the episode, ostracized me for doing what I thought
was right. This was my first real experience with strangers
who unaccountably wanted to hurt me.

In my sophomore year, I was living in relative isolation, and
perhaps that is what took me away from my studies and toward something new—the *Drakonian*, the college's weekly
newspaper. I was not a good athlete, although I've always
been drawn to sports for their metaphorical richness. I tried
to join the drama club, but I was blocked, or so I was told, by
an acquaintance of Kip's; and Kipist forces also blackballed
me in every fraternity, even the one that admitted outcasts.
The *Drakonian*, though, slowly welcomed me, and for the
first time at Darleigh, I felt a sense of belonging and purpose; I spent hours in the paper's soiled basement offices,
tapping out stories on the keys of a gray Underwood with a
sticking *K*, and much of my junior year passed by there. I

cannot say that I respected most of my associates; in truth, I became numb with boredom when one of them brought up yet another issue of alleged interest to our school. But a few of us were excited by the world beyond Old Drake, and I felt this especially with Carol Ann Margolies, a Jewish girl who wore a J.F.K. button in the middle of her blue cashmere sweater. Carol Ann was not only a gifted reporter, but had a probing intellect; I itched to become closer to her.

By the time our senior year began, in the fall of 1960, Carol Ann and I shared a similar contempt for what T. S. Eliot once called the "confused cries of the newspaper critics and the *susurrus* of population repetition that follows." I recall particularly the night that a dozen or so of us got together in our darkish "newsroom" and watched Kennedy debate Nixon as we chewed on slivers of an immense pizza covered by pepperoni, sausage, and anchovies. When the hour was over, and our group had dispersed, only Carol Ann and myself were left, lingering on the couch, four or five curled slices of cold pizza lying in the box. As I remember, we sat silently for a while, and as I watched the button winking from her sweater, I had a sudden impulse: Although endorsing a candidate would breach generations of *Drakonian* tradition, I wanted to support Jack Kennedy.

Carol Ann's lips twitched, for she was far more nervous than I at taking such a step without consulting the others. I remember that as we sat together on a bench and I typed, my arm would now and then brush against her cashmere sweater. I do not think this was intentional on either her part or mine, but as I wrote words I've since forgotten (now and then smacking the flawed Underwood, with its *K*-less ennedys), I felt aroused and guessed, from Carol Ann's breathing, that her plumpish body was affected, too. It was my first experience of this sort (her panties were ripped in our heated hurrying), and it was an ironical coincidence that this occurred on the day of my debut column.

Not surprisingly, several on the *Drakonian* staff protested; some went so far as to insist that I resign or they would. I believe that I was right to stand my ground, although I wish the others hadn't quit in such a snit. Had I left, I could not have given myself a column. Had I not done that, I would not have discovered at such an early age the heady rewards of writing one.

* * *

My family lived in Buffalo, sooty and robust in the days of my serene childhood in the late forties and early fifties. My father was a successful insurance man and my mother was rarely happy, except while tending to her garden, which surrounded our comfortable little house on Cleveland Avenue.

My father held strong, favorable opinions about the Democratic Party, and his plump face would redden when I questioned his judgments about such men as Averell Harriman and Herbert Lehman, as well as figures like Joseph Crangle, who helped to run Buffalo; and sometimes our arguments at dinner became so fevered that he would leave the table. Still, I respected my father as the sort of white-collar personage who forms the spine of America. (He lived, as Max Weber once said, in the belief that "a man does not 'by nature' wish to earn more and more money, but simply to live as he is accustomed to live.") My parents were people from whom a kind of wisdom may be distilled—that is, if one listens carefully. I cannot say that I agreed with most of what I heard from my father; nor, in any case, do I remember very much. But growing up as his son undoubtedly helped me to become the person I am.

I graduated from Darleigh in the spring of 1961 (my senior year clouded in a haze of sensuality; often, Carol Ann Margolies and I sat side by side, and found ourselves caught in nature's urgent grip, shedding garments even as final sentences were composed), and as soon as I got my diploma, a magna, my father asked what I intended to do with myself. We'd held similar conversations over the years, and I had always tried, while being tactful, to make clear that I had no intention of following his example. When I mentioned a career in journalism, I saw despair distort his features, so I quickly went on to explain. "I don't intend to be the sort who rushes all about and writes about fires and crime," I said. "I intend to write about the fabric of our time."

My father shook his head. "Someday you'll want to marry, to have a family," he said. "I know one newspaperman, Fred something-or-other, who bought a whole-life policy from me. I believe that Fred earns ninety dollars a week."

I suppressed a chuckle. "I believe that Mr. Walter Lippmann earns many times that amount," I replied, and went on to mention several others who did, too.

My father had no good answer at the ready, and said, "You've got big ideas, Brandon."

My father, as I've tried to suggest, had a good heart, but he was not quite able to comprehend what mattered to someone like me and frequently repeated his small-minded belief that I had "big ideas." That was certainly true, but I also understood, as Napoleon said, that ability is of little account without opportunity. In any case, I'd heard about an opening at a Buffalo newspaper from a high school acquaintance (someone who had not gone to college, and worked in the sports department). It was not a prestigious venue, but I believed that I would have a chance to learn the "ropes," in a way that might not have been possible elsewhere.

The *Buffalo Vindicator* was on Main Street. Carved above the doorway in Gothic type was the newspaper's name and in the lobby was a mural forty feet long and fifteen feet high. It contained, among its many elements, a rendering of Thomas Jefferson reading a newspaper, alongside Theodore Roosevelt and Abraham Lincoln, doing likewise. In the background was the great dome of City Hall, and Lake Erie, and if one looked closely, it was possible to see countless skillfully painted windows and through them more people reading more newspapers. It was a sight listed in guidebooks of the time, and the image has undoubtedly influenced my thinking about the profession.

My city editor, Julius Portino, was, like myself, a native Buffalonian. He had sleepy brown eyes and soft, drooping bags beneath them; and he told me that starting reporters got paid seventy-two dollars a week and were expected to write about fires and crime. Portino clearly was content to spend a lifetime with the *Vindicator,* and to respond to news without trying to understand its deeper import. I was struck by his utter lack of curiosity.

I had been on the job for two or three months when it occurred to me that an inordinate number of fires were breaking out and that a larger story might be lurking behind the many smaller ones. Portino, however, merely shrugged when I went into his office and told him this with the fervor of a young reporter. "There are a lot of frame houses in Buffalo, Brandon," he said, and lighted another of his many cigarettes. "Some of them burn."

Julius Portino had been drafted after high school and had gone to Korea, an experience that certainly shaped his view that the unexamined life is greatly to be preferred. We were, beyond a doubt, from two different worlds, and I believe that if we had not disagreed about the fires that kept breaking out around the Queen City, something else would have led to a clash.

What precipitated the break between us was my decision to speak directly to his superior. Even now, I can visualize Wriston (Chet) Budge, who had been the newspaper's editor in chief since 1935: with his shredding unlit cigar, the ashes that made their powdery way down his unbuttoned vest, and his reddened, gray cheeks, it was as if he had shaped himself into his idea of a small-town newspaperman. Mr. Budge had won a Pulitzer Prize for deadline reporting in 1928, when he was, like myself, a recent Darleigh graduate. I think that this shared background helped us to forge a bond, although Mr. Budge by the time we met was in his middle fifties. I had also heard that he was disappointed at his lot in life, and he often complained that writing editorials for his Buffalo readers had become an unwelcome chore.

I proposed to Mr. Budge that I pen a series of commentaries on the outbreak of possible arson. There would be no reckless claims (I stressed the word "possible"), but we would ask for increased vigilance from the fire department, the police, and the mayor's office. As I went on, Mr. Budge seemed barely to pay attention, yet he also seemed overjoyed at the prospect that I would be willing to jot down my thoughts; and before I'd finished laying out my thesis, he clapped his hands with enthusiasm. Moments later, he summoned the city editor to join us.

I was horrified at Julius's display of uncontrolled anger, particularly when he turned to me, in front of Mr. Budge, and said, "You went over my head, you fuckface sneak." I could not meet his eyes, nor could I watch the spittle at the corner of his mouth, and my gaze drifted over to Mr. Budge's Pulitzer citation, which hung alongside his Darleigh diploma.

"I told our young friend," Portino said to Mr. Budge, his teeth quivering, "that he ought to do a few months of reporting before jumping to ridiculous conclusions." I noticed that his face had become darker. "But our young friend appears to prefer going behind my back."

I understood how he could have reached that conclusion, but I was nevertheless stunned. My ambition, after all, was modest: to examine a puzzling situation, and to put authorities on notice—trying, in short, to do my job. I did not know what Julius Portino's private agenda was, or even if he had one (as far as I knew, his Italian family, although it imported olive oil, was upright), but his words made me suspect his motives.

"That's a curious statement," I said, looking directly at Mr. Budge, who looked at his watch.

"Look," Mr. Budge said, "I haven't the time for this, but what is there to lose, Julius? Why don't you calm down?"

Portino seemed unable to speak. Nor did he say much more to me during the time that I remained at the *Vindicator*, although now and then I thought I heard him mumble curses, and it was clear that he would always regard me with irrational anger.

There was another reason that I chose to begin my career in Buffalo: the chance to lodge in my childhood home, which allowed me to become better acquainted with my parents while setting aside money that would otherwise have gone for rent. But after six months, it came to a stop; my mother wept, and it's probably true that, in my zeal, I might have taken too little heed of others. (In some ways, my own son has mirrored my conduct of that time; I've not been able to avoid thinking that a certain portion of just deserts has been served up.) In my case, there were the usual small things that widen a family's gulf: Often I was required to use the car, and it was not always convenient to let my father know in advance. The telephone sometimes rang at hours that neither my father nor mother, who kept to a regular schedule, could become accustomed to.

I most regret making use of my father's confidential in-

surance records, which contained invaluable data that supported my thesis on the arson epidemic. To this day, I believe that we had an implicit understanding, but I can also
see that I might have misread him and might have misjudged the reaction of his former clients. Those who have
wished me ill have ferreted out this episode and made much
of it, as if it revealed something fundamentally bad about
my character. Those who know the facts will see that it was
a terrible misunderstanding, although for my father, who
was dismissed from his job for cause, the consequences were
severe.

I did not make many new friends during this time in
Buffalo. I had nothing in common with my former classmate—the one who worked in the sports department. His
first love was hockey, which bored me, while mine was baseball: an expanse of greensward excited my senses, for it
promised not only a game, but a representation of life. At
night, I often thought about Carol Ann Margolies, with
whom I'd promised to stay in touch. I remember sending her
a Hanukkah card, and thinking how grateful I was to have
learned about her ancient faith. But life, I have found, is a
series of partings, and regrets; and when one is young, one
quickly meets new people who seem to replace the old ones.

*　*　*

When I moved out of my parents' house (my unemployed father was blenched and silent; my mother turned away), I found a small apartment in Allentown, Buffalo's Greenwich Village—a place with bookstores and boutiques and soiled antiques. It was, all in all, a happy period, for my career had taken an important turn. Although my suspicions about an arson spree were widely denounced, I had struck an anxious chord with readers. This attention persuaded Mr. Budge to let me hone my analytical skills, a chance that falls rarely to today's crop of journalists.

I was also learning another basic technique of journalism: that extending the hand of friendship may lead your fingers into the pocket of revelation. (For example, I became attentive to an older woman in the newspaper's personnel office and, from her, learned the retirement dates of several colleagues.) One must, in short, be able to relate in a human way to men and women of lesser ability and diminished circumstance.

In those days, my hair, which became prematurely pale, like my father's, was a shiny yellow. Nor had I put on the weight that, regrettably, I've added over the years—the result of many repasts in the best restaurants of the world. I say this as a roundabout way of observing that women found me physically attractive, and also seemed to sense in me a lifetime teacher.

One of these was Lisa O'Rourke, who worked in the local office of Buffalo's most important congressman. Ignaz Mscislowski had been returned to Washington for nearly thirty years by loyal constituents of Polish extraction. Because Mscislowski had served for so long, I thought that he would be wise in the ways not only of western New York, but of the world, and I made it a point to seek him out whenever he was in town, which was infrequently. Soon, however, I had another reason for repeated visits to Mscislowski's office (a small suite close to the famous golden-domed bank on Main Street): Lisa had shiny black hair, a full figure, and a laugh that put dimples on her rosy cheeks. One warm day, I recall, I was passing through her neighborhood in south Buffalo (then as now an Irish enclave), and saw her in shorts, freckles on her upper legs, mowing her lawn, and I briefly persuaded myself that I was infatuated. But what is infatuation? Certainly not a subject that lends itself to easy analysis by an aging columnist; as Emerson put it, "The natural association of the sentiment of love with the heyday of the blood seems to require that in order to portray it in vivid tints, which every youth and maid should confess to be true to their throbbing experiences, one must not be too old."

My nature has always been solidly heterosexual, and I'm certain that tracings of desire go back to elementary school. I also believe that the subject of sexual attraction is not something to be dwelled upon, even in memoirs as open and honest as these; yet I recognize that one's appetites and encounters are inevitably an important part of life, and to leave out the firm breast, the moist coupling, the soft descent of lips, would be unfair to readers. That applies not only to myself, but to what I know about the private lives of public figures.

It was not long before Mr. Budge generously agreed to let me attempt an occasional column, which ran with a tiny photograph of me alongside it. When I study my aspect, glancing from crumbling paper, I see a prideful expression that was perhaps unwarranted. But when I read my words, I rediscover a thoughtful mind. In the spring of 1962, for example, I saw Fidel Castro for the preening dictator that he was. I predicted the eventual importance of Barry Goldwater, and was sympathetic to Negro aspirations. Like any newspaperman, I remember carrying fresh, inky copies of the early edition to my apartment, where I would warm a pot of tea and turn to my byline, aching with pleasure.

When Lisa O'Rourke agreed to spend an evening with me, I planned an itinerary that would begin with dinner and then a spin across the Peace Bridge to Canada (to enjoy the lights of the Queen City) and back to Allentown, where we could stroll the picturesque streets and stop for a drink at the Teddy Bar. (The Teddy Bar, long since demolished, commemorated the installation of Theodore Roosevelt after the assassination in Buffalo of William McKinley by an anarchist of Polish extraction.) From there, I imagined, I would take Lisa to my apartment.

It was a spring day—a surprisingly balmy evening in early May—and, as it turned out, it began with a dinner that unfolded just as I had imagined: linguine with clam sauce, a small salad, a carafe of wine—very modest, but we shared similar tastes. After that, Lisa wanted to see a movie—I think it was a film by one of the gifted Italians so popular at that time; we drove to the other end of the city, somewhere past Hertel Avenue, with its Jewish shops and historic Hebrew letters. All the time, we found we had much to talk about: of leaving Buffalo (and moving to Washington, Lisa to work on Capitol Hill, and me to a newspaper). We talked of literature—and of Kennedy and Governor Rockefeller. As we watched the movie, my brain swimming with the wordy subtitles, I let my arm drape across her shoulder and felt her warm body shift slightly toward mine. My fingertips tingled.

My car was a 1955 Chevrolet two-door, turquoise and white with assertive chrome hillocks. (Can America build such machines today?) As we drove about, the springlike air almost hid the somewhat rotten stench that sometimes drifted from the waters of the lake, and I probed, though very gently, for some secrets about her personal life. I recall that I sustained a painful erection throughout our conversation, and that when I told Lisa about my friendship with a Jewish girl at Darleigh College, she turned away, as if in embarrassment. When she told me that she'd been in love the year before with a Catholic boy who still lived in Buffalo, a banker, my face reddened with jealousy. Then, when I moved toward the next phase of my plan and asked her to accompany me to the Teddy Bar, she looked at her watch, wound about her delicate, pale wrist, and exclaimed that the hour was late and that she needed to be home. Lisa lived unselfishly with her widowed mother, which made me feel fonder of her. When she leaned to kiss my cheek, I became dizzy with longing.

I recall all this in detail, because my columns after that showed a new vigor. I suspect that my unspent sexual energy affected my work and I became adept, for the first time, as a phrase-maker. Sometimes I fell into the weakness of being clever for cleverness's sake, but at other times people thought that I was unusually keen. Several times I got a note of praise from Mr. Budge, and a few words, such as "Good work, Sladder—insightful!" were enough to brighten my day.

The most notable columns were about Congressman Mscislowski. Not only was he a skilled legislator, with an instinct for serving his constituents; he was also someone with an appetite for luxury. That was my reluctant conclusion after numerous visits to his office and one strained conversation with the congressman himself. To Lisa's credit, she never doubted her boss's probity. It was in fact a source of some tension between us, just as it was a matter of tension when she refused at first to let me see his records. For it had come soon enough to that: I'd begun to visit Mscislowski's office to see Lisa, but almost without realizing it, I then began to be more interested in the congressman.

Although Lisa was a few months my senior, she knew far less of the world than I did. Nevertheless, I *was* immensely fond of her—never more so than on the June day when she surrendered more than Mscislowski's confidential files. I remember that we drove to Niagara Falls, a place that was surprisingly neglected by Buffalonians, and that we found a spot in the woods for a picnic. My memory is that Lisa wore the same shorts that she'd worn on the day I'd seen her mowing the lawn; I wore my favorite pair of rumpled khakis, a cotton Oxford shirt, and sneakers. I remember tugging at her clothing with clumsiness, and yet with the urgency of youth, and of the shock I got when I exposed to daylight those parts of her that heretofore had been secreted from my view. Later, when our passion was spent, she told me for the first time that she thought she might love me. I treasured her words and attempted to reciprocate them, while feeling vaguely uneasy and thinking, for the first time, that Lisa in sunlight looked quite ordinary.

In the days and weeks that followed, our relationship, such as it was, became strained. When I inquired more frequently about Ignaz Mscislowski's private life, Lisa would recoil, as if I'd struck her. When I asked about a safari which the congressman had taken through Kenya (he had bagged a wildebeest, the skin of which was stretched across a wall of his office), her expression told me that I'd hit a nerve. I shook my head when I told her that I must write about these things—and ask Mscislowski about these matters—because I was a journalist. It was my duty. Paragraphs of indignant disclosure welled up within me.

Mscislowski himself, in our single conversation, showed himself to be a man of exceptional crudeness. I asked him politely about his expensive cars, his large houses in Washington and on Lincoln Parkway, his voyages. In my most diplomatic voice, I asked how that related to his work. "You little college-boy shit," he said, and seemed almost short of breath. "You write that and, I swear, I'll carve you a new asshole."

I replied that history would be the better judge of that, to which he answered with more crudity. When I repeated the thrust of our dialogue to Lisa, hoping for her applause, she wept, despairingly, for she knew that the congressman would blame her. I murmured something I'd come only vaguely to understand: that truth is a stern master and sometimes it forces us to hurt those we care about a lot.

* * *

One morning in the summer of 1962, I realized that it was time to get out of town. A number of things had, very quickly, gone wrong: My parents were no longer speaking to me, and my father, a proud man, refused my offer of financial assistance, although I would not have been able to afford very much. My situation at the newspaper was not happy; my youth and ambition undoubtedly grated on others, as did my increased influence in Buffalo's civic life. Ignaz Mscislowski telephoned Mr. Budge to urge my dismissal, and Mr. Budge, to his everlasting credit, ignored him, but I got little support from Julius Portino, the vengeful city editor. Nor was I treated well by Lisa O'Rourke who, having lost her job with the congressman, suddenly changed careers and took a job in Lackawanna, in a steel factory. (Today, after an unsuccessful marriage, she is a paralegal in Syracuse, and has two grown children of whom she is no doubt justly proud.)

I thought constantly about my professional future, although I had no real prospects; I felt enclosed by Buffalo, its lake and suspicions, and viewed any intellectual diversion with disproportionate gratitude. When Mr. Budge, showing continued faith in my work as a commentator (and pleased by my clearheaded thoughts during the Cuban Missile Crisis), asked me to accompany him to Washington for a conference on containment, I seized the chance.

It is hard in the modern age to imagine that Soviet expansionism was once an important topic, but that was very much the case for quite a long time. Not without good reason. If anything, history has taught us that our fears were justified, and today I regard my own writings on the subject with considerable satisfaction. My critics have called me overzealous, particularly in respect to my repeated calls for stern military action in various trouble spots; and perhaps the United States was right not to intervene in every case. But as I've frequently counseled, one should consider a baseball game when it is the bottom of the ninth and the bases are loaded and the score is tied. Should one wait passively, hoping for a walk, or swing away?

I had never actually been to Washington, but I remember that from the moment of my arrival—when we crossed the Memorial Bridge and saw the Lincoln Memorial, which, as Mr. Budge pointed out, not only resembled the Parthenon, but was in far better shape—I felt that someday I would matter here. As our taxi took us past the Ellipse, then the White House (the Capitol's dome was bright in the near distance), my eyes could barely focus; by the time we reached our destination, the Mayflower Hotel on lower Connecticut Avenue, I unashamedly confronted my ambition to live here.

"We're here to learn, not to play, Sladder," Mr. Budge cautioned me several times, although I thought I detected mischief in his eyes and a hint of eager anticipation in his open mouth and flushed face.

"It's thrilling to be here, Mr. Budge, and I'm immensely grateful for the opportunity," I said, or words to that effect.

I longed to call Wriston Budge by his nickname, "Chet," but did not dare to do so without an invitation. Yet I welcomed the chance to grow closer to him, for he was not only my patron and mentor at the *Vindicator*, but, to my good fortune, the most powerful person at that institution.

"We should always welcome the opportunity to learn from important people," said Mr. Budge, and once more I spied that glint of mischief as he licked his lower lip.

Our seminars were held in a lower ballroom at the hotel, and the panelists presented a pantheon of that era. Robert (Bob) McNamara spoke of our national goals, and I saw the weight of decision on his shrewd, smooth face. Mr. Budge and I sat together, and as he chewed upon a shrunken cigar, sometimes lighted and sometimes not, I watched his gray and red cheeks and veiny nose grow brighter. The day became long and I felt a little restless, although occasionally I would take notes when a speaker said something unusually sound. More than once, Mr. Budge whispered that I should plan to write about a topic under discussion, and I was grateful for his confidence.

At night, we found that there was not much to do. We did not know the other guests, although Mr. Budge appeared to have a nodding acquaintance with a few journalists, who vanished long before the panels were concluded. (One, I learned later, was either Arthur Krock or C. L. Sulzberger.) The streets of the city were dimmer than the streets of Buffalo; it was as if shadows hid within shadows. On our first evening, Mr. Budge suggested that we dine at Harvey's, and there I had my first glimpse of J. Edgar Hoover, seated in a booth with a male friend. Afterward, we retired to our room, which seemed alarmingly cramped; a tiny table separated two narrow beds. Mr. Budge had told me that we would share lodgings in order to save money, but I worried about snoring, of committing a faux pas in my use of the toilet (I wiped up each drop, in my eagerness to please!), or of letting slip a remark that might alter his opinion of me. As our visit was to consist of only two nights, however, I persuaded myself that the time would pass quickly and interestingly. As it turned out, both wishes came true, although not in ways I could have anticipated.

*　　*　　*

I had been listening to a fascinating panel discussion about the Captive Nations of Eastern Europe (a matter of considerable interest to us because of Buffalo's large population of Polish heritage) and was surprised, after half an hour, to find that Mr. Budge had not taken his usual place by my side. At first, I'd not noticed, for I'd napped briefly due to my loss of sleep (Mr. Budge's snores had been of unusual duration and shifting volume, and he smelled not unlike my old college roommate, Kip). It was not that I missed his sidelong glances and his taps upon the program, which was his way of showing approval, but it seemed odd to be there by myself. After all, I was in no position to take a hand in shaping the issues under discussion; nor did it seem useful to me to question the panel without Mr. Budge there to witness my query.

What I remember feeling (or so it seems to me today) was a sudden rush of disquietude, a sense that something untoward might have happened to Mr. Budge. I suspected nothing unlawful; Washington in those days was not the crime-infested place it has become. But I feared that he might have been felled by an accident (slippage in the bathtub, I'd recently heard, had led to the breakage of my father's arm) or perhaps a seizure of some sort. I knew that such fears were probably unjustified, but with those human concerns in mind, I discreetly made my way out of the crowded ballroom and found the elevator that would take me back to our carpeted floor.

I cannot remember what I'd hoped to discover in our room, other than this: I had hoped to find it empty, and thereupon I would return, feeling relief, to my seat in the ballroom. As it turned out, though, the room was occupied, in the fullest sense of that word. Mr. Budge was seated upon the same bed in which I had passed a fitful night, and he was naked and white and furry. Nor was he alone. In the place where I might have expected to see his middle parts, I saw a great mass of red hair, cascading over a back that was embraced by the strap of a black brassiere as well as by Mr. Budge's spotted hands. I was not yet familiar with the practice of fellatio, but it became obvious that Mr. Budge was an enthusiast. I, myself, could do nothing; and, after taking in the scene (to this day, I remember the milky white skin of the woman in black undergarments and the insistent movements of her head), I fled. In moments, I was once more listening to a deputy secretary of state discussing the importance of the survival of a free Berlin (the Soviets, I believe, had been threatening again). But I could barely pay attention; I kept thinking back to the tormented expression on Mr. Budge's face and I wondered what we would say to one another when next we met.

In the event, our conversation was brief.

"I believe I shall head back tonight to Buffalo," Mr. Budge told me in a whisper, when he'd returned to the hard chairs of the ballroom, where the fifth panelist was giving his extremely interesting views on Eastern Europe's prospects.

My face must have shown disappointment; Mr. Budge could not have known my true feelings.

"I would very much like to stay for another day, for I am

learning so much," I said, hesitantly, knowing that I would be able to make some inquiries about future employment.

He nodded, almost as if he did not care if I remained even longer than that.

"Of course you'll stay, Brandon," he said, a rare use of my first name. Then he looked at me closely: "And of course you will be discreet. I want your solemn promise."

Our eyes met in a moment of raw emotion.

"Of course," I said. "Of course, Chet."

* * *

Whenever I retrieve certain moments from what Augustine called "the great palace of my memory," I am struck by how much one learns in a lifetime, such as the simple truth that one should leave a place where one is unappreciated. So it happened in Buffalo, where now, after our excursion to Washington, even my reliable patron, Wriston Budge, appeared to harbor a quiet hope that I would go away. More than once he raised his voice to say, "Goddamit, stop calling me Chet!" If I entered a room and tried to initiate a discussion on issues affecting Buffalo or the nation, Chet would twitch as if an electric shock were being administered.

The winter of 1962 was bleak. My father had taken a job at a grocery store (by chance, I saw him stuffing paper bags, his eyes reddened, and I ran off, unseen and ashamed).

After the holidays, which I spent alone, I decided to leave regardless of my prospects—to sail off, so to speak, without safe harbor. In some abbreviated accounts of my life, my choice is cast in romantic terms; and in some ways, admittedly, it was brave simply to pull up anchor. Yet my opportunities in the city of my youth were, as I have hinted, dwindling. It is unlikely that I could have learned much more from Chet, and when he said to me, "Look, Brandon, I want you out of here for your own good," he seemed to mean it.

When I gave notice, I took some small satisfaction in the astonishment on the faces of my superiors. As I bid good-bye to the hostile city editor, and saw his soft, brown eyes and sagging skin, I felt only pity, for I knew that Julius Portino—jealous, impotent, supremely untalented—would never move beyond the radius of his desk, thick with mediocrity, orbited by a tiny solar system of similar desks. When we shook hands, our eyes did not meet, and they would, we both knew, never meet again. (When the *Vindicator* was bought years later by a newspaper chain, Portino was one of the first of the old guard to hit the pavement. The news did not surprise me, but I sympathized with him and wished him well.)

With Chet, it was more difficult. He had, after all, been a friend and benefactor. I had but two small favors to ask: a letter of credential and a few months' salary to tide me over. He appeared anxious to help, and as we shook hands, solemnly, I remember patting his shoulder and blurting out, "Don't worry, Chet, I'll never tell a soul." Inexplicably, he turned away with a grimace, and said something that sounded like "You blackmailing son of a bitch." I was puzzled by his attitude, for I'd entertained the naive hope that he could see into my heart and know better; and looking at Chet, moments before passing the huge, fading mural in the lobby for the last time, I felt bruised by his suspicions and wondered how long he'd harbored them. The answer (which I never learned) might explain the unkind things that he said about me in the years before his timely death.

Within days, I was on a Greyhound, speeding toward Washington (the icy, black hills of western New York giving way to the red bricks of Williamsport and the fields of Gettysburg). For much of the fourteen-hour journey, I slept, imagining for myself a new life, thinking, like Cervantes's hero, that "the brave man carves out his fortune, and every man is the son of his own works." I remember most of all a feeling that returning to the nation's capital was inevitable, and that good things would come of it.

I had brought in my suitcase a book by Walter Lippmann, my letter from Chet, and a determination to succeed. My mood was intense and unsettled as the bus entered the city and we drove past the warehouses of New York Avenue; and as I walked through the doors of the Greyhound terminal, with its pinball machines and smoky lunch counter, I noticed that the winter air was milder in Washington. But I shivered from the moment I stepped outside, perhaps realizing that it was a very short walk from there to the White House.

I made my way around much as a tourist would, and on my first day found a place to live near Dupont Circle (a dark room with a sink and shared bath in the back of a Victorian brick row house on O Street), a neighborhood that reminded me in some ways of Allentown. I spent an excessive sum on a wardrobe: a dark-blue suit from Lewis & Thomas Saltz; a shirt with French cuffs from Garfinckel's; an Italian necktie, and English shoes. Even at a young age, I knew that I needed to present myself as a serious person.

Soon I found myself spending considerable time in the vicinity of the Capitol, and came to recognize the faces of members of Congress, as well as a few journalists, who were set apart by their irreverence and ill-fitting clothes. I was eager to know them, for in my spare time, I had been leaving résumés with some of their employers, but they regarded me as if I were an interloper. One man with a superior expression (I believe that he worked for the *Baltimore Sun*) would ask me where Buffalo was, and where I had bought my suit. I tried to smile at such hazing, hoping that it would be accompanied by camaraderie, but soon enough I came to see that I appeared as something of a nuisance to almost everyone.

Sometimes, when I watched my peers race about, it felt hopeless; when I walked past newspaper buildings, such as the *Evening Star,* I thought of returning to Buffalo, although Chet and others had hinted that my position would be filled within moments of my departure. As my money petered out, I spent my days somewhat aimlessly, visiting museums, going to afternoon movies, attempting to meet editors who might take a chance on me, and having no luck.

On one of these days, I came to know a young Englishwoman whose name was Zoe Wicksworth. We met on a late-January afternoon, at a bar on Pennsylvania Avenue, not far from the Capitol. I was in a booth, reading a newspaper and sipping a bottle of Schlitz (a taste I never acquired), and sensed that I was being watched. When I looked up, I saw Zoe, who had mouse-colored hair and a sad, vanishing expression; her brows rose over large brown eyes as if to ask a question, and when I nodded a tentative yes, she crossed the room to join me.

I did not then suspect that she was a woman for hire; I thought that she'd found my blond, wavy hair and boyish features attractive. I was quickly disabused of this notion when she sat beside me in the booth, skillfully moved her small hand to my privates, and whispered, "That'll be ten dollars if we go to my place." I nodded. In those days, people who behaved promiscuously did not fear AIDS or the growing assortment of vile diseases that now make their way from person to person. It was then the custom to slip on a rubber, as we called it, and plunge ahead without fear of consequence, which was, above all, an unwanted pregnancy. I am in no way condoning such behavior, but events transpired in a far more innocent fashion than would be possible today. In the case of Zoe Wicksworth, I quickly became aware that she might become an invaluable source, so my motives were mixed.

Because I intend this to be an honest account, I admit that on the evening that we met, we repaired to her room on Eleventh Street, Northwest, a place even more dismal than mine, which contained a mattress losing its soiled innards, occasional bursts of steam in the radiator, and no decoration apart from a photograph of two depressed adults, whom I took to be her parents. We agreed on a sum of seven dollars, for which, it turned out, I had purchased one service. When I was evidently satisfied, she turned to me with a shy smile and asked, "Was it nice?" Not wanting to hurt her feelings, I replied that it had been, and when she suggested that we could try it again in the near future, I did not summarily dismiss the possibility.

"The gents from Congress like that best," she told me. "With the mouth," she added, unnecessarily.

"Do you have lots of gents from Congress?" I inquired, my focus suddenly shifted.

"Lots of very famous people let me do them," Zoe said. "I usually never get young blokes like you."

"You like 'em young, eh?" I said.

"I like 'em quick, is what I like," she said, and with that she sat beside me, aware of my keen interest in her thin body and budlike breasts. My response was quickly apparent, and on this occasion, for a single dollar, she did me with her hands.

It was in the course of one of these visits a few days later that a thin, handsome young man with light brown, curly hair and glimmering blue eyes stood at the door as I was leaving. He was a Missourian of about my age, who had come to Washington to study law at the George Washington University. It was clear that he, too, had been befriended by Zoe; unexpectedly, his first reaction at the sight of another young man in her company was a warm greeting and an exchange of gentle laughter. His name was Bob Hudnut—the same Bob Hudnut now known to anyone who follows American politics. We were destined to meet frequently over the following decades, and in increasingly intimate circumstances; and not surprisingly, I was taken by his charm from the beginning.

It was clear to me that Zoe had considerable knowledge of American politics. In the hours we spent together becoming friends, she would often shake her head and laugh with wry amusement. "If only they knew," she would say, and to that I would say, "Knew what?" She smiled as if in possession of a secret, and nothing I said could persuade her to yield it, although I told her that she could be of immense help to my career and I twice favored her with a small box of candy, a Whitman's Sampler. It was only after several weeks of visits—and an expenditure of nearly five hundred dollars, depleting my funds almost entirely—that Zoe told me that she could arrange to have me meet someone I must still identify as Deputy Secretary X.

"He said he'll talk to you, but I got to do him special," she said. Her accent had become thicker, and when I kissed her on the lips in gratitude, I saw that her eyes were a little teary. I wondered, vaguely, what "special" meant.

This is a roundabout way of saying that my patience with Zoe was rewarded, for, in truth, the services she offered to me—which had consumed so much of my savings—were becoming less than satisfactory. Yet she took pride in her work, and I sensed that it would be insulting to express anything short of complete pleasure. I'd also come to suspect that Zoe's feelings for me had become more tender than businesslike ("You poor bloke," she would whisper), and I knew that her willingness to introduce me to this Deputy Secretary X was inseparable from this sentiment.

When I met Deputy Secretary X on a warm night in February (the January thaw had come late), I knew that he was not eager to talk to an unemployed journalist whom he did not know and had no reason to trust. He was, rather, somewhat nervous, and it was no accident that he had asked me to call on him after midnight; only one light was on in his three-story Federal house on Thirty-first Street and he let me in quickly.

He seemed surprised by my appearance, for I must have appeared, even in my best clothes, a very young man. But soon he offered me a glass of port and, as we spoke, I relaxed, admiring his carpets and paintings. There were sparks in the fireplace; a book of poems by Auden lay carelessly open on a small table. He smoked many Chesterfields and told me that he had known Chamberlain and Churchill, Roosevelt and Truman, Hitler and Stalin, and had amusing stories to tell about all of them. He evidently had never read anything I'd written in Buffalo, because he asked my views on Berlin and Kennedy's evolving relationship with the Soviet Union and listened intently as I expressed thoughts that had been suppressed for weeks: that Kennedy was a man who was just reaching his stride and that Khrushchev gave every sign of being a more interesting Soviet leader than might have been expected.

It was only toward the end of our conversation that Zoe's name was spoken aloud. When I said, softly, how valuable she had been to me—and that I knew how very much her "special" talents had meant to him—he patted my knee, and looked stricken in much the way Chet Budge had once looked stricken. He quickly asked what he could do to help me, and I could not contain my gratitude: I told him that I sought only his advice, as well as an occasional introduction. There were, for instance, rumors about Americans going to war in Southeast Asia, and perhaps he could tell me things in confidence. He several times called me "my boy," and shook his head.

Deputy Secretary X, so far as I know, stopped speaking to journalists soon afterward. But he shared insights of immense value and importance with me (which enabled me to write with some authority), and I treasured him at once as a new champion. Through him, I made several invaluable contacts and attended social events that, coincidentally, led to my acquaintance with two future employers. But although Deputy Secretary X remains alive and mentally alert, he has always been too busy to reply to my letters and good wishes. I regret that we have fallen out of touch, but he will understand, if he reads this, that his secrets—all of them—are safe with me.

*　*　*

Whenever I glance at keepsakes, such as a photograph of myself with a leader, I think about fate. What if I'd not met Deputy Secretary X and gone on to write an article about American power? What if I'd not sent my essay to *New Terrain*, the legendary journal of opinion? Fate, after all, is what separates a glorious fly ball from a mediocre home run.

In the early sixties, *New Terrain*'s importance far exceeded its circulation, and in my letter to its editor, Tobias Goldenstein, I said that nothing would give me greater pleasure than his approval (and reminded him that just the other day I'd met him at a cocktail party). What I'd sent him was a document that probably exceeded six thousand words—twice the usual length for *New Terrain*, but appropriate to a subject of this complexity.

There followed an excruciating wait. On several occasions, while trying to gather fresh information from Zoe Wicksworth, she was quick to notice my distraction. "When you can't get it up, it's like you're not here," she said, although she would eventually have her way with me. At one point, I became so uneasy that I took myself on solitary rambles through Rock Creek Park, imagining myself in the company of Henry Adams, but also Lippmann and Krock, whom I had quoted in my article. At times, I wondered if the work I'd been so assiduous about had been lost, and if I should retype it from my smudged carbon. Each afternoon, I would stop by my depressing room and ask my landlady, with increasing fear, if mail had arrived for me. These inquiries were eventually greeted with impatience by the landlady, who once had been invisible and now seemed querulous. I noticed that she had three rather large wens on her double chin, and that her buttocks were enormous. I vowed that I would move from this place as soon as possible.

I remember still the great thumps of my heart when, on an afternoon in March of 1963, my landlady, with a suppressed smirk, handed me a large envelope with the familiar *New Terrain* logo (a steam locomotive) embossed on the upper-left-hand corner. It was terrifying; when I saw the thickness of the packet, I knew that it contained my manuscript, perhaps with a brief, dismissive note from Tobias Goldenstein, and feared that our relationship would end before it could begin. I smiled with a confidence that belied my fright, and walked to Connecticut Avenue, clutching the envelope as I strolled past a Hahn's shoe store and a movie theater and then made my way along N Street, to a bar where I ordered a Schlitz and sat down, prepared to face the worst. My hands trembled.

What it contained—I will now end the suspense—was my manuscript, but one that had been transformed by the practiced hand of a great editor. My sprawling essay had become an elegant survey of American foreign policy, perhaps one third of the original size. And attached to it was a message on *New Terrain* stationery, the locomotive steaming along the margin. Among my more precious documents (those I will include in papers I donate to Darleigh College) is this note: "Hope you find this acceptable. T. G." Acceptable! Even thirty years later, I remember the thrill that those words gave me, not to mention the check for one hundred and fifty dollars. With the impatience of youth, I found my way to a telephone booth (I believe it was outside a Peoples drugstore) and burbled thanks to the woman who answered. My excitement was only magnified by these appended words: "Come see me the next time you're in the neighborhood."

My life had been an oddly solitary one, broken by encounters with Zoe, to whom I still extend my arm in gratitude, but few others. Deputy Secretary X might suggest a social event, but always seemed eager to end our conversations. I had lost touch with my parents, who never responded to my friendly postcard.

The offices of *New Terrain* were a block or so south of Dupont Circle, on the third floor of a town house on Connecticut Avenue, their single doorway marked by the locomotive logo. When I arrived, I was greeted by a young woman whose blouse was a sheer white fabric. I note this seemingly irrelevant fact because, as my gaze drifted there, she smiled knowingly and said, "I keep track of people who watch my bosoms." I tried to laugh easily, but stopped when she said, "I'm Esther Goldenstein, the boss's daughter."

I managed a confident smile. "I'm Brandon Sladder," I said, "and I am here to meet your father."

"Oh, you're the one who sounded so insanely happy on the telephone," she said, and laughed in a tinkling way. I noticed her large white teeth and rather full lips. Esther Goldenstein was, I could see, about my age, and as I studied her more closely, I realized that she was enormously attractive. What was more significant was that she appeared to find me attractive, too. I wondered if, like Carol Ann Margolies, she was Jewish, and tried to remember if Passover had come and gone.

"Daddy liked your article, but I had no idea what you were trying to say," she said. "I like your hair."

I ignored this personal observation, for I wanted her to grasp my ideas. "I was trying to explore the resolve of the West," I said, pleased to see that she was paying close attention and that she seemed to understand my thoughts as they poured from me. "I think I've gotten a clear sense of the ways in which we're headed for problems," I went on. "For example, hardly anyone is paying close attention to the evolution of the Common Market, or the determination of our enemies in Southeast Asia—I'm speaking of Laos and Cambodia and Vietnam. This is serious business."

"You're so grown up," she said, and shook her head. Her

thick dark hair looked soft. Then she arched her back slightly. "Where are you living?" she asked.

When I told her, she replied, "We live in Georgetown. That's where Jack Kennedy lived before he got to be President. That's where lots of the most interesting people live, the people who run things. You should live there."

Of course I knew what Georgetown was—I would have loved to tell her about meeting Deputy Secretary X. I will also confess that, as we spoke, I permitted myself a brief erotic daydream that involved her breasts.

"It's important that you know people," she went on. "I could tell from your article that you've met all sorts of important folks."

I was impressed by her intuition. I sensed that we were destined to be friends, and that made me happy. I think it was at that moment that Buffalo—Chet Budge, Julius Portino, Ignaz Mscislowski, Lisa O'Rourke, my parents—suddenly seemed so far away as to be another planet.

Moments later, Tobias Goldenstein himself came into the reception area; from the instant he extended his hand—a surprisingly small and hairy limb—until we'd finished our initial conversation, I can remember nothing. He was not a tall man, perhaps five-nine, and bulky without being fat. His white hair was combed flat over a grand, somewhat flushed head, and he had a slim nose and wide mouth, a curious combination that seemed to confer upon him an exotic authority. I shuddered with nervous pleasure.

"I'm so very pleased to be here, sir," I said. "I've just been talking to your daughter."

"Esther likes giving advice," he said, and chuckled.

"She's told you where to live by now, I'll bet, and where to shop and how to vote."

I nodded, still nervous, and I could sense that Esther took pleasure in my awkwardness.

"We're a small operation," Tobias went on, putting his small hand on my shoulder, guiding me through the only doorway to a row of offices that made up the central nervous system of *New Terrain*. It was only then that I realized that he was offering me a job—a most desirable internship. He told he that he regretted not being able to pay more than sixty dollars a week, but pointed out that, for two years, I could write regularly. It was, he said, "an opportunity not without value." I do not believe I had ever felt such intense happiness.

I was given the smallest of the billets, at the end of the hall. Next to me was Lionel Heftihed, the literary editor, who I judged, from his dismissive wave (he was chatting on the phone), to be an arrogant sort. One office down was the widely admired John Wilson Stapling, the chief political writer, who had been there longer than anyone. Stapling's office was dark, but I peeked inside and gasped at the powerful mixture of gin and tobacco smoke. In the corridor just outside his door, I saw that the mustard-colored carpet had tiny burns where cigarettes had been ground out.

"Here's what you'll need, and not much more," said Tobias, pushing me back toward my new office. He waved at a pine desk, a Royal typewriter, a pad of paper, and a telephone with a gash in the plastic. "By Friday week"—we were speaking on a Tuesday—"I want three thousand words on Kennedy's record as a civil rights president."

At that moment, my first doubts about my new position began to gnaw, ever so lightly. My views on J.F.K. and civil rights are well known by now; I later wrote (in one of my most-quoted lines) that he "lacked the convictions of his courage." This, however, was not a subject to be ordered up as if it were a hamburger, but an opinion to be cooked like a casserole. Although I have never deviated from my view that Tobias was a great teacher (and even today I sometimes hark back to his example), I was shocked at the haste with which he wanted to take his stands. But for now, in this storm of bliss, I put aside my doubts.

*   *   *

In my good fortune, I walked about a little dazedly, and I remember stumbling across streetcar tracks, the ruins of an earlier, lost city, and finding myself surrounded quite suddenly by men and women in flashy clothing who happened also to be black. I was fascinated by the great distance I sensed between their lives and mine, and moved quickly westward, toward the shops of downtown, and then to more familiar spots: the R.K.O. Keith's theater at Fifteenth and G streets, the Treasury Department, and soon the White House, looking through the fence that lines Pennsylvania Avenue. I imagined Kennedy inside, and entertained the thought that he would see what I'd written for New Terrain and summon me for a talk. A little later, as I passed the Mayflower Hotel, I felt the rattle of memory. Then I looked up and down Connecticut Avenue, breathed deeply, and was, immediately and buoyantly, at home.

A few days later, with help from Esther, I found an apartment on P Street, east of Wisconsin Avenue, with a sunny living room, a small bedroom, and a showerless bath, which rented for eighty-four dollars a month, a sum I could barely afford. It was to be my home for the next three years, and certainly Esther's ardor sealed my decision. She jumped with encouragement when the landlord left us alone and then she impulsively leaned toward me and kissed me on the lips. "Oh, take it," she urged. "You'll be happy here, I promise you!" Her kiss affected me, and when we repeated it, her friendly, warm body lingering a few seconds beyond a standard hug, she no doubt felt solid evidence of my excitation.

It was hard to resist her tiny enthusiasms, and I had no idea that her mild attraction to me had become a full-fledged infatuation. In some ways, she reminded me of Carol Ann Margolies, although Esther was not a practicing Jew and, to my disappointment, had no plans for Passover.

Now I can understand why my article on J.F.K. did so much to launch me as an analyst of the American scene. In the spring of 1963, however, I could only regret the difficulties it caused in my relationship with John Wilson Stapling, the venerable political writer.

I had written at blinding speed, and what I'd pointed out—and what seems obvious now—was that Kennedy had no Negro friends to turn to for advice, and that his relationship with Martin Luther King, Jr., was uncomfortable; they were, I wrote, "two politicians separated by a common language." I argued that Kennedy could not advance the nation's civil rights agenda until he came to terms with his own ambivalence and suggested that he visit the Negro sections of his city—our city—and, in E. M. Forster's famous dictum, "only connect." (I would repeat some of these themes that August, at the time of Dr. King's famous march.)

I was astounded at the response I got for this prescription, and when I asked Tobias Goldenstein about all the angry letters, he gave me a reassuring smile. Of course I was stung by correspondents who called me "simpleminded," and a "nitwit," but I was delighted to have stimulated a debate. With John Wilson Stapling, however, it became almost personal. I was particularly wounded by his cutting suggestion that I had not done adequate reporting to support my thesis.

By the time I met him, Stapling—Johnny to his friends—was a sad wreck of a man. His gray hair was rarely combed and his flushed cheeks were often covered with gray stubble. Several of his teeth were green, and not well anchored by his gums; white hairs grew from his ears, like pale cilia. Often, he reeked of gin, if not vomit, and his voice was usually slurred. He wobbled when he walked, and his prose had become flaccid. I say this not to denigrate his character or his work, but to give an accurate picture of a man whom many regard as one of the foremost commentators of the mid twentieth century.

Mencius, the Chinese sage, asked, "How can one get the cruel man to listen to reason?" For months, I made what must have been pitiable attempts to win Johnny's approval. I would knock on his door, and leave instantly when I saw him hunched, in his characteristic slumped stupor, at the typewriter. I would ask for his impressions of Rusk and Mc-Namara, whom I had seen only from afar, or of historic figures he had actually known, such as Nicholas Longworth. I once asked his advice, for an article with which I was struggling, on the risk we were taking in simply abandoning Laos. But he seemed unwilling to meet me even halfway.

Nevertheless, I admired him. Perhaps, in the years that I knew him, he was no longer the man he had been; perhaps his work lacked the insight, the language—the near brilliance—that had once distinguished his reportage and analysis. But one had to respect him for what he had accomplished, and when others mentioned his work, I always spoke of it respectfully.

Lionel Heftihed, the books editor, was another matter. He was then in his mid-thirties, which seemed to me a fairly advanced age (I am amazed to think that I was not yet twenty-four), and yet he still wore his crimson Harvard sweatshirt, as if he were a youth. Lionel's dark hair was combed back in a lofty wave and his teeth gleamed. His obsession then (for Lionel was, above all, a dilettante) was German romanticism, and it puzzled Tobias as it puzzled me that the Schlegel brothers, Friedrich and August, made so many appearances in the magazine, a trend I once referred to (this irritated Lionel) as a "union of the unfathomable with the unreadable." I'd thought it was a pity that Lionel took so long to apply his natural intelligence to matters of interest to the rest of us, but when he finally did begin to concentrate on issues, there was something childlike about his attempts, despite the stabs of insight that would slash through the cloth of his turgid argument. When my essay on J.F.K. and civil rights appeared, Lionel complimented me, but I knew that he had not read a word of it, and that he rarely read anyone but himself. These differences aside, Lionel and I might have become friends were it not for a personal matter that I will explain later.

The most generous encouragement came from Esther, who also had talent as an editor, although not as refined as her father's. Whenever I wrote, she would volunteer to help and eagerly scan my words, often proposing a change that seemed so right that I was embarrassed not to have made it in the first place. I loved to watch her pencil, homing in on the poor phrase, the flawed metaphor, giggling merrily when she saw that it pleased me. "You're so close to getting it right," she often said, squeezing my hand when I nodded with gratitude.

In sum, I was in a state of equipoise, lifted by the optimism of that time (even the cherry blossoms that spring had a special glow). Quite often, I would walk the mile or so from Georgetown to my office, not realizing what soft delusion enveloped us. In the evening, I sometimes went to the baseball stadium that had been built on the easternmost part of Capitol Hill and watched the Washington Senators. When they took to the field and engaged in the rhythms of the game—hope and patience, longing and despair—I would feel at one with life.

*　　*　　*

One sad note was Zoe Wicksworth, whom I hadn't seen since I'd gone to work at *New Terrain*. But on the day I moved my few possessions from my room near Dupont Circle (Esther had let me borrow her father's Oldsmobile station wagon), I'd gone back alone to pick up several last items, and saw Zoe: She was leaning against the sharp prongs of the cast-iron fence in front of the row house, wearing a silk skirt and a low, thin blouse. In the sunlight, she looked small and unwell; I saw blemishes on her face that I'd never noticed, and a pale beige birthmark just above her breastbone. I silently thanked God that Esther was not here.

"So you got new digs?" she said.

"Larger than these," I told her. "I have a new job, Zoe, and it's a very good one. I feel very fortunate—especially fortunate, and grateful."

"Oh that's real nice, it is," Zoe said, and for a moment she did look genuinely pleased. "I've been missing you, Brandon."

I attempted to reciprocate with a few words, but, to judge from her expression, they fell short.

"You know how I feel about you, Brandon," she said. "You know it's different for you. That's why I got my friend to meet you. You know I'll do you any time."

I could not bear to look at her then, because her eyes were reddish and, curiously, filled with tears.

"I appreciate that, Zoe, I really do," I said, and when her pale face pressed against my shoulder, I patted her back, which felt cold and moist in the warm, dry air. I quickly lifted my hand.

"Who was that helping you move your belongings?" she asked.

"Just a friend, Zoe," I said, wondering how long she'd been watching. "A girl who works at my office."

She stared at me in a puzzled, awful way and said, "I'm dead, aren't I? For blokes like you, I'm dead."

The more I tried to reassure her, the less I succeeded, and moments later, Zoe walked swiftly off into the quiet grayness of my new city. Two or three times, she looked back, but I pretended not to see that, although I did.

* * *

I did not develop many lasting friendships in my first year or so in Washington, but several people came to mean a good deal to me. One was Madeleine Whitbridge, who was unfairly labeled a "Georgetown hostess," but was in many ways a wise woman with a subtle grasp of our city's secrets.

My name had been given to Madeleine by a thoughtful Deputy Secretary X, and she kindly included me among a group she called "my novices," mostly young people who were new to town, among them several up-and-coming journalists, lawyers, and politicians. In this community, I became ever more persuaded that rewards naturally fall to the most accomplished. It is, to be sure, an imperfect system, as I once remarked to Gerald Ford, but, by and large, I believe that that is the way things ought to work, and that is what I wrote when the subject, as it invariably did, arose.

Madeleine lived on Q Street, in a detached brick house surrounded by the sort of garden that is becoming rarer in Georgetown. Her late husband was often described as the "swashbuckling veteran of the O.S.S.," and Willy Whitbridge's operations in the Middle East remain legendary. (When I think of the bungling of our modern C.I.A., I wonder if even someone like Madeleine's husband could restore its sense of mission.) When Willy Whitbridge died in a boating accident in the Tidal Basin, in 1951, she emerged, after a period of mourning, with a personality of her own. She was tall and exceptionally thin, and had, I always thought, a storklike gait. She must have been in her midfifties when I met her on a bright early evening in May (the azaleas were brilliant, the dogwood gone), but her hair was white and she'd begun to wear the wide silver necklaces that were a trademark.

When I introduced myself, she said, "Ah, Jack Kennedy's civil rights adviser!" and chuckled merrily.

"If only he'd listen," I replied in self-deprecating fashion, seeing by her quick smile that I'd won her over. She gripped my arm tigerishly with her brown-spotted fingers, and said, "You'll do, young man, you'll do!"

There were perhaps thirty or so of us, and for two hours we circulated, reaching for bits of food carried on wide silver trays by Madeleine's two faithful servants. At every sound of her gay, knowing laughter, I was drawn to her, but held back, perhaps out of shyness, perhaps because others pushed forward to listen to her observations. Later, at other, similar gatherings, she introduced me to people who would play vital roles in my life; on this occasion, I recognized a handsome youth with glittering eyes. I could not at first recall his name; then I remembered that I'd met him in the dingy room of a young Englishwoman whose name neither of us wanted to speak aloud. This was Bob Hudnut, who had just graduated from law school and had taken a summer job on the staff of a United States senator from Missouri. When Madeleine saw that we appeared to know one another, Bob Hudnut explained (as I mouthed an assent) that we had a mutual friend.

"I've been impressed by your work for the magazine," Bob said, and nodded several times.

I wanted to know more, for I believed that I was already acquiring what we call a "voice," but when I asked Bob what article he'd liked best, he seemed unable to make a selection; and in any case, the subject rapidly was forgotten when Madeleine introduced us to a young woman with blond curls and large, hazel eyes. Her name was Gretchen Furlong, and her beauty unnerved me, so much so that I will confess to following her about from room to room in order to string together fragments of meaningless conversation. I can't recall a word that we spoke, but in bed that night, I was unable to sleep, tossing about with a desire known to all young men; and, as I solved the problem at hand, I wondered whether I had ever met anyone so charming and whether I had made a favorable impression.

Quite apart from Gretchen's beauty, her pear-shaped breasts, and luminous skin, I felt that she possessed a sympathetic hardheadedness, as well as a sense of humor equal to my own. I was grateful when Madeleine Whitbridge, two or three weeks later, arranged a dinner party at which I was seated next to Gretchen.

From that evening, we seemed to find common ground. She said that her older brother had gone to Darleigh College, and I realized that I had known him, although vaguely, as an athletic, personable young man with casual good looks. She asked about my work at *New Terrain*, then told me that she knew Lionel Heftihed, although her eyes took on a curious blankness when she spoke his name. During the soup course, I felt her knee brush mine and it remained in close, warm proximity until the coffee.

It was a giddy, bright table for eight, including Senator Jasper Munroe of Kentucky, a centrist Republican with whom Madeleine obviously had formed a close friendship. Madeleine did everything with style, from candles on the table to the witty conversation that she led. We covered a great deal of ground that night, speaking not only of Castro, but of Khrushchev and of Goldwater's chances. There was, I still remember, much laughter at the imagined strains between Kennedy and Lyndon Johnson, and a debate over a column by Lippmann which had appeared in that morning's *Washington Post*. I remember feeling . . . not envy, exactly, but something far more positive: a belief that someday people would discuss something that I'd written with the same lively interest.

As for me, I was engrossed by Gretchen Furlong. I watched her golden hair tremble and saw what I imagined was ironic intelligence in her greenish-brown eyes. I learned that her father had done something in the State Department under President Eisenhower, and that her mother raised horses. She also revealed that her parents, despite being Republicans, sometimes saw the Kennedys on social occasions. The more we talked, the less I could conceal my interest in her, and I jiggled my knee.

I am afraid that I was a poor guest, for I neglected the others as Gretchen leaned toward me and said that she was rarely in Washington on weekends. Her parents, she went on, had a farm in Warrenton, Virginia, where she kept an Arabian jumper. When she asked if I rode, I dissembled slightly and told her that my enthusiasm was tempered by my physical remove from rural America. At that, she promised to invite me to Lorton Hills, as their farm was called.

"I don't believe you really like horses, for no man I know ever does," she said, with what I found to be a bewitching smile.

"I may not like them, but I can see their purpose," I assured her, which made her laugh. "They also represent for me the romantic imperative," I added, pleased with my coinage. She looked puzzled, prompting me to continue: "If I don't like them personally, I like what they represent in myth and in the movies."

With that, we were off on a discussion of Westerns, and in particular the television program *Gunsmoke*, a dialogue that everyone overheard and which prompted enthusiastic confessions.

"I just love that show to death," Senator Munroe said with a chuckle. "I like Miss Kitty," he went on, and fastened a toothy smile on Madeleine. "You remind me of Miss Kitty," he said, and the table erupted with laughter.

I was pleased to have begun this conversational gambit, one that included all of us, and I could see that my hostess was grateful. I hope I've made it clear that I was fond of Madeleine from the first, and saw her as considerably more than an entrée into Georgetown society. In my note to her the next day, accompanied by flowers and inadequate thanks, I complimented her on the brilliance with which she'd chosen her guests. When I telephoned several days later and asked if I might stop by to chat, she was enormously receptive. She also said, in a sly voice I had not heard before, "You want to talk to me about Gretchen, don't you?"

It was true that my thoughts then were focused on Gretchen, but my body was more in touch with Esther Goldenstein. When I arrived each morning at the magazine, she greeted me from her perch at the reception desk. During the day, she would find her way to my office, and, due in part to her superior editorial skills, I welcomed her visits.

Let me emphasize that the fault for what happened between us was entirely mine, and also that I was immensely fond of her. There are times, when I hear a certain sort of laughter, that I expect to turn and see her fresh white teeth and shiny black hair. I expect to hear her say, "Stop being such a horse's ass, Brandon!" or "Is that some Buffalo expression?" At certain moments, when I am shopping for clothes, perhaps picking out a tie, I expect Esther to weigh in. I took pleasure in her company, for she was a true friend and guide. More than anyone, she helped me to feel that I belonged, and it bears repeating that her instincts for sinuous prose were a professional blessing, although her father was my guidepost; to this day, Tobias's influence may be found in every sentence that I pen.

I told myself that I had yet to "cross a threshold" with Esther, although I cannot deny that I received physical pleasure from her, and it would be naive to claim that when she visited my office, I expected no more contact than a blue pencil. Nor can I deny that my colleagues, notably Johnny Stapling and Lionel, suspected that Esther and I were having an affair, and I worried that they would share their suspicions with Tobias.

The first crisis came several weeks after I'd gotten to know Gretchen, and had joined her for a weekend or so at Lorton Hills. I had by then purchased my own jodhpurs and boots, as well as a tennis racket and an overnight bag made of buttery leather. I seemed to have an affinity for horsemanship. Sitting atop the rippling back of a steed, guiding it into a canter with a gentle kick of my heels as flies buzz about, is enormously satisfying. As a people, we Americans have come far from our sturdy frontier past; I doubt that one in ten could build a cabin, skin a deer, or, for that matter, change a set of spark plugs. I believe that I surprised the Furlong family with my enthusiasm for this sport that puts one so in touch with our fabled past.

I knew that I disappointed Esther whenever I had to leave the city for a weekend (I hinted at visits to my ailing parents in Buffalo), but matters always returned to normal on Monday; if Esther knew where I'd been, she gave no sign, and it was not her nature to ask. In any event, the time came—inevitably—when I had to break a firm date in order to spend a weekend at Lorton Hills. I have always made it a rule to honor social engagements, but sometimes another opportunity is so alluring that one simply has to breach etiquette. That was precisely what happened when Gretchen told me that the Kennedys were coming to dinner, and that Jacqueline Kennedy might wish to ride. It was, Gretchen knew, a last-minute invitation; she realized that I might have another engagement and would understand if I could not accept.

This was a torment because I had already agreed to accompany Esther to a dinner party that was to be given, apparently, in my honor—in other words, my semiofficial welcome to Washington and to the magazine. In addition to Esther and myself, the guests were to include Tobias, and Johnny Stapling, to whom Esther had been talking, urging him to be more generous and to share his accumulated wisdom with me, and a few thoughtful men in official positions, all with their wives.

"It will be such fun!" Esther had said a few days earlier, with a bold kiss. "Everything in Washington gets done at parties. I want people to know you the way I do. I want them to like you." She paused and smiled mischievously. "You do seem just a wee bit pompous and arrogant to some people, you know."

On some level, I know that I committed a faux pas by my last-minute cancellation; yet the other option, in retrospect, would have been much worse. The alternative to insulting my colleagues at *New Terrain*, and the putative host of the dinner party, and, I suppose, Esther (whose gasp of sadness, when I hurriedly told her that "something extraordinary" had come up, gave me real pause), was this: I would have missed my chance to meet J.F.K., a few months before such a meeting would no longer have been possible. I cannot say that Jack Kennedy and I became intimates in the course of our evening at the Furlong farm; after all, I must have seemed quite unimportant. I believe, though, that from the moment of our handshake in the Furlongs' living room, we understood one another.

I'm often asked about Kennedy, and I realize that, for most Americans, he has receded into history's mist. Ugly things have been said about his private life and some of his policies have been questioned. But of what President is that not true? In any event, after the introductions (Jackie soon admired a pair of recently acquired Hepplewhite tables), I had my first conversation with J.F.K. He asked me about Darleigh College, and said that he'd often driven through Old Drake, and once had dated a Darleigh coed. When I told him that I had endorsed his candidacy in the *Drakonian*, he grinned broadly and said, as I recall, that victory has a thousand parents, but defeat is an orphan. At that point, Jackie nudged his elbow and pulled him toward a guest who had just arrived, Jasper Munroe of Kentucky. The senator was accompanied by Madeleine Whitbridge, and I was very pleased to find myself suddenly among old friends.

Jasper, like Madeleine, must have been fifty-some years

old, but to me, with his reddish skin and watery eyes, he seemed of an ancient generation, far removed from that of the President, who looked like a statue with perfect chestnut hair. I tried throughout the evening to get closer to Kennedy, in order to continue our talk. I was eager, for example, to seek his views of the impending demonstration led by Martin Luther King, and also to quiz him on the status of Berlin in the aftermath of Cuba. I had by now acquired a more somber view of the world; my sense of Soviet intentions had darkened in recent weeks. I had gotten to know one Russian diplomat, Boris S., who shook his head with foreboding and turned away whenever our paths crossed, and I was eager to share my impressions while they were fresh. But at dinner, Gretchen was seated on my left, and Madeleine on my right, and my efforts went into entertaining both of them while trying to overhear snippets of conversation from elsewhere.

The very cozy dinner for ten included two guests who arrived late: a cultural emissary from France and his attractive, spirited wife. I took an instant dislike to the Frenchman, with his short, dark, New Wave hair, and was baffled whenever I heard his smooth, Gallic whisper bring forth gentle laughter from Jackie, who spoke the French tongue. At one point, he asked the President if he planned to meet again with Chairman Khrushchev, and I heard Kennedy give a noncommittal answer, accompanied by his attractive grin. During one exchange, I missed something that Madeleine had said to me, and I sensed her annoyance when she guessed that my attention was elsewhere. My solution was to speak quickly about the beauty of Lorton

Hills, and in particular the formal dining room, whose walls included portraits of many Furlong ancestors, all in the style of Rembrandt Peale. As Madeleine's eyes took in the sur- roundings, I could see that her agitation was calmed. Gretchen, who wore a white dress that was somewhat im- modest in its cut, merely glowed with pleasure.

Before I knew it, the evening was over. The Kennedys left first (I remember a bright white flash as someone took a photograph of us), their departure signaled by the thrilling sound of a helicopter, chop-chop-chopping. We all took the opportunity to say a few words, and I could not resist the chance to ask J.F.K. if he was aware of my critical yet sympa- thetic article about his civil rights policy. "I tried to be prag- matic, but I wanted to inject a note of caution," I said. Then, as I tried to continue the conversation, I noticed that Jackie had a somewhat impatient look. She'd made it obvi- ous early in the evening that she had no wish to speak to me. "I'm sorry I missed it," Kennedy said, fixing his strange blue eyes on me, his bronze face composed as we communi- cated silently. "I'll ask my staff to get me a copy." It was the last time I saw him alive. I never learned whether he kept his promise.

* * *

People in the middle of the action find it difficult to keep a secret. Everyone, for example, seemed to know that I'd been to a small dinner with the Kennedys, and while I could not conceal my pleasure at having been there, I was mindful that others could find it hurtful—especially Esther, who had heard rumors of my interest in Gretchen Furlong and had begun to regard me with anguished stares. Her father, quite understandably, was also disappointed that I'd so suddenly changed course on the night of a dinner that was to welcome me to Washington. A vague, undefined chill made its way into our working relationship, although that in no way diminished my respect for Tobias.

It is hard to re-create the emotions of another time. As I stare from my study and watch the peregrinations of a few scrawny birds, I find myself remembering the Friday that

Kennedy was assassinated (I'd just come back from a solitary lunch and sensed a curious stillness in the street). I recall feeling many things, including a powerful wish to call Gretchen—to share memories of the evening we'd spent with our leader. When I couldn't reach her, I wandered the corridor at *New Terrain*, sharing my grief with Johnny, Lionel, Tobias, and Esther. It was, we knew, our duty to make over the magazine, which was scheduled to go to press that evening, and we met in Tobias's messy office, stumbling over piles of books.

"It is as if a great athlete has been cut down in his prime," I said, and they looked at me with astonishment. "As if Ted Williams was stopped in midswing. The game goes on—the demands of history assure that—but joylessly."

Tobias looked, I thought, strangely impressed, his eyebrows aloft; I saw that Lionel was nodding vigorously, yet seemed unable to stop nodding. Esther's wide lips parted as if to express a thought. Johnny Stapling, as if overcome with emotion, left the room.

"The shocked crowd does not like the pinch hitter," I continued. "We cannot boo, because we know that he did not enter the game on his own volition, yet we resent him. Just minutes before we were watching someone else and the world was right."

It became clear from their approving silence that these thoughts would be included in the memorial edition of *New Terrain*, and I took notes even as I uttered them. After that, we all fell to work, producing articles of which I remain proud. Tobias wrote the lead essay, followed by Johnny's assessment of the political scene and Lionel's valiant, if inco-

herent, attempt to give Kennedy's presidency some historical context. I believe that my essay (perhaps because of its
universality) encapsulated the sense of loss the nation felt.

Later, in my office, I was joined by Esther, her face still
damp with tears. "I'm so upset, I'm so upset," she said, repeating herself to the point where it became hard to concentrate. But I wasn't dismissive. The truth is that I had not
behaved nobly toward Esther. Even when she knew that I
was seeing someone else, I tried to assure her of my continued affection, and it remained difficult to control my natural drives. To put it bluntly, despite her misgivings, Esther
offered herself to me like a gift, which I greedily unwrapped.
When she asked if I liked her, or perhaps loved her, I told
her that I certainly did, but I was unable to tell her that she
could never give me what I wanted most. I am ashamed to
say that our physical union was completed on the floor of
my office at about midnight on the day of the tragedy in
Dallas. My hands gripped her soft thighs, and in the midst of
my fiery release, I worried whether our nation would keep
Kennedy's pledge to bear any burden for the sake of liberty.

During most of the next year, I became a regular guest at
Lorton Hills, so much so that the Furlong family began to
regard me with a critical eye, as if realizing for the first time
that I might become one of them; or, rather, that their
daughter might become a Sladder. Gretchen's parents expressed some eagerness to meet my family, and even suggested a weekend jaunt to Buffalo. Unfortunately, my
mother had suffered a series of strokes, and had been con-

fined to a wheelchair, or so my father said in his short note. That made any chance of a relaxed family gathering out of the question, and the Furlongs quietly accepted that decision. I was of course proud of my parents. I'll say again that my understanding of the backbone of America came from watching my "old man" sell insurance and, in adversity, bag groceries. I admired my mother's staunchness in the face of a life that could not have been wholly fulfilling.

I wish that they could have shared my happiness. As Gretchen and I cantered in the Virginia landscape, it sometimes occurred to me that in Washington, a mere forty miles away, people could so easily lose touch with nature. I felt content, and I believed that Gretchen and I had fallen in love. On an early summer day in 1964, not long before the national political conventions, as I fed an apple to my panting horse, I asked Gretchen in a firm voice to be my wife. Moments later, she dismounted and accepted me wholly.

Among the memorable people I came to know at Lorton Hills was Gordon Gallatin, the editor of the *Washington Telegram*. (Or, I should say, know better, for I had shaken his hand at one of Madeleine's soirees.) There are those one meets in life with whom one feels instant rapport, and that is how I felt at the instant I spoke with Gallatin, whose friends called him Beano, and whom I called Beano within an hour of our meeting.

Photographs of Beano show the dark hair, turning to gray, and the fine, aquiline nose with its slightly flared nostrils. But one cannot see in these portraits the knowledge of

Washington in every word he uttered. He was then, I suppose, about forty. He had been with the *Telegram* since the days of the Korean War, and realized that much still needed to be done in order to rejuvenate his newspaper, especially the editorial page.

"It commits the crime of being dull," I said, with the tactlessness of youth.

"You've hit the goddam nail on the head," Beano replied, in his colorful way.

"What people forget," I volunteered, "is that no idea means much if it is not expressed well."

Beano roared with laughter, and so did I, with pleasure. But I have noticed that pleasure is often accompanied by pain, although it is not necessarily pain for the person who experiences the pleasure.

Gretchen's parents often seemed discontented: Her father, while serving on many corporate boards, missed the chance to serve the nation as he had under Eisenhower; her mother was incapable of discussing anything but horses; and both Furlongs appeared to regard me as some sort of interloper. Gretchen's brother, Preston, on his rare visits to Lorton Hills, could not conceal his dislike, and once asked me if I had known a friend of his from Darleigh, a man named George Kipler III, who was now a stockbroker. I denied it, and only later realized that he must have been referring to the unfortunate Kip.

By now—months before a notice appeared in the *New York Times*—news of our unofficial engagement was becoming known. Madeleine Whitbridge, already a loyal friend, declared that she would give a garden party in our honor. In the course of that summer, several of Gretchen's friends gave dinners, and teas, and for a very long time it felt as if we were the toast of Washington.

My writing, all at once, was being quoted, and some of what I said aroused enmity. I saw, for instance, that the future of the Republican Party wasn't going to be determined by the likes of Nelson Rockefeller, and I expressed this view without equivocation. And while, as I wrote in that same summer of 1964, there was much to admire about Robert Kennedy, I was not among "the emotional throngs who needed to be hosed down" after he spoke at the Democratic Convention in Atlantic City. After that, Johnny Stapling stopped speaking to me altogether.

My articles about Lyndon Johnson won plaudits even from those who did not agree with me, and I was among the first to predict that his defeat of Goldwater would be disproportionate. I was not always right; for instance, my early support of the "domino theory" in Southeast Asia (heavily influenced by Deputy Secretary X) was undoubtedly a tragic misjudgment. But my views became steadily more knowledgeable and assured; and although I could not pretend to have achieved the stature of a major journalist, the more I wrote, the more my circle of friends and acquaintances widened. During the long Thanksgiving weekend, when I twisted my ankle in a spill from a nasty horse, get-well cards arrived from several people I'd never met, including a number of congressmen. One of these was a particular surprise. It was from a Republican who had managed to win a seat despite the L.B.J. landslide: Bob Hudnut, the young man I had first met in Zoe Wicksworth's room, had suddenly returned to Missouri to run against an aging incumbent, and had defeated him.

William Hazlitt has observed, "Those who wish to forget painful thoughts, do well to absent themselves for a while from the ties and objects that recall them," but that proved to be impossible. When, eventually and inevitably, Esther Goldenstein learned that I was to be married, she said, with undisguised distress, that I had not been altogether honest with her.

My reply was more in the way of explanation than excuse: I confessed that I'd fallen in love with Gretchen Furlong—suddenly, unexpectedly, and genuinely. That did not mean that I was indifferent to Esther, I said; and as I told her this, I could see that she appeared to believe that she could win me back.

"She's a spoiled rich girl who cares more about her ponies than anything that is real," Esther said, and I noticed that her bosom was pointing at me, as if accusingly. "The truth is—my father is right—you want to marry a social better."

Those words were perhaps the most hurtful she had ever uttered. I have heard them many times since, and over the years I have become inured to them, but at that moment I was wholly unprepared for such an insinuation.

"No, Esther," I replied, with hot frankness. "I want to marry someone with whom I feel entirely at ease on an intellectual and social basis."

"You're so foolish sometimes, Brandon," she said, and I was surprised at the way she looked at me—not angrily at all. "I really think you're someone who thinks it's better to express an opinion than actually to have one." In her eyes, I thought I saw a mixture of pity and affection, and she laughed—a little too loudly, I thought. Yet both of us knew that our relationship, such as it was, was over; or, if not over, on hold.

*   *   *

I never understood why the owners of *New Terrain*, a
wealthy middle-aged couple, closed the magazine. After
all, it was losing very little money and there were many po-
tential buyers. I never spoke to them personally (they lived
in New York), but my suspicion is that they had become fa-
natical. They told people that *New Terrain* had strayed from
its mission and that they preferred euthanasia to a lingering,
ideological death.

They were particularly upset, I later learned, by my essay in cautious praise of the Federal Bureau of Investigation.
Tobias, shaking his head, had told me that he loathed every
word I'd written, but published it out of respect for the con-
trarian principles of the magazine. (I have never allowed
the essay to be reprinted, but my thrust, in brief, was this:
that we Americans ought to be grateful for what I called,

paraphrasing Emerson, our "blessedly foolish consistencies," and in this category, I singled out the F.B.I., with its corps of lawyers and accountants, and pointed to its ideals and accomplishments—in other words, its happy consistency.) Today, I would have phrased some of this differently. I certainly wish that someone had told me that our owners had once been investigated by the Bureau because of their ties to an undeniably left-wing club (an affiliation that ended before I came to the magazine). I realize that it serves no purpose to revisit that moment, but I could be accused of intellectual cowardice were I not to acknowledge the scars on the arm of my past.

After that, my working conditions—which were bad enough after missing the dinner in my honor—swiftly worsened. Johnny Stapling, of course, had long stopped speaking to me, but he was usually sopping drunk. I learned of Lionel's seething anger from a conversation with Madeleine, who said that he blamed me personally for the demise of the magazine. Tobias, who seemed almost to shrink and his spidery hands to darken, never lost his gentlemanly demeanor in my presence, but we found little to talk about. (I had never broached the question of becoming a permanent employee when my internship ended, and I shall never know if it would have been possible.) Only Esther opened her arms and offered me a consoling hug when we heard the news on a Friday afternoon in April of 1965.

"My God, what are we going to do?" she said.

Her softness pressed against me, and when she smiled into my eyes, I felt the ache of melancholy.

"It's a rotten turn," I said.

"I don't blame you," she said. "You have to write what you have to write. And I suppose I can't even stay mad at you, even though you hurt me terribly."

I looked into her widened eyes and assured her that hurting her was the last thing I had ever wished to do.

"I hope you won't forget me, Brandon," she said, somewhat mysteriously.

I promised that I wouldn't—"How could you ask such a question of me?" I said—but I could not really concentrate on what she was saying and can barely remember it. Unlike my colleagues, I was not despairing, but almost joyful; and what gave me buoyancy, despite the dreadful news, was the knowledge that my own future was bright. What I knew, and they did not, was that I had been summoned to visit Gordon Gallatin at the *Telegram,* and had every expectation that Beano (who evidently remembered me from our stimulating conversation at Lorton Hills) would offer me a position.

As it turned out, it was another week (anxious, silent) before I actually saw Beano; when I arrived at the *Telegram*'s turreted building on Pennsylvania Avenue, not far from the Capitol, I paced the sidewalk, breathing deeply, going so far as to avoid cracks in the pavement. Now and then, I glanced upward and thought, in Marlowe's phrase, of a place "whose shining turrets shall dismay the heavens." When I arrived at the fourth-floor editorial department (the elevator had creaked and seemed not to move), a matronly woman guided me to the editor's office, so swiftly that I barely took note of the newsroom, a flickering of sound and paper. My nervousness receded only when I saw Beano, whose hair had become a little grayer in the months since I'd seen him. He held out his fine, large hand and greeted me as if I were an old friend, for indeed he had that uncanny way of making you feel that you had known him all of your life.

"That's a goddam shame about your magazine," he said, immediately putting me at ease with his earthy language. I found that we were sliding back into that easy rapport of our first meeting.

"It's fucking sad," I replied, in a sorrowful voice that captured my mood.

"Poor Tobias. And Johnny," he went on, as if to himself. "No one will give him a job."

"It is a fucking pity that he's a lush," I agreed.

Beano shook his distinguished head in a way that I thought resembled that of his ancestor, Albert Gallatin, whose picture was behind him on a wall. Also on that wall were framed editions of the *Telegram*, with headlines that announced Lindbergh's flight, the atomic bomb, the Dallas murder, and other souvenirs of the twentieth century. I tried to keep the demeanor of a casual visitor, but my heart was astir. Nothing, I realized, would mean more than to be offered a job, and therefore Beano was, at that moment, as important to me as Tobias had been two years—two whole years!—earlier. I remembered that, at Lorton Hills, we had discussed the newspaper's opinion pages, and I had expressed my honest view that they were tedious. Suddenly, he grinned.

"What the hell do you want to do?" he asked, with his famous directness. He went on to tell me that they needed a police reporter for the District of Columbia, and another one to write about suburban Maryland.

My heart shrank: I was an analyst of domestic and foreign issues; and although I had become experienced in "hard news" in Buffalo, I worried that my lack of interest in small, local subjects might offend Beano.

"I'm enormously grateful that you would go out of your way to see me," I said, choosing my words with care. "My fear—and at this point it is only a vague fear—is that my fucking talents might lie elsewhere."

"It's pretty obvious that you like being a thumbsucker," he replied, and for the first time, his eyes were not quite so warm.

"You see right the fuck through me," I replied, essaying a grin. He tilted back in his large chair, then leaned forward, his head pushing toward me.

"You're going to marry the Furlong girl," he said, suddenly. "She's trouble, if you ask me. Spoiled. Rich. Not all that bright."

I was nonplussed at this sudden, blunt assessment, for in fact the wedding was only two months off. Recently, I had been thinking that Gretchen was a little too giddy with excitement to suit my sober mood, but I told Beano none of this. Rather, I said, "I am very fond of her."

"Look, the Furlongs are old friends," Beano said, still leaning forward, his eyes on mine. "And she is goddamned attractive, too. Great pair of tits."

I could not suppress a smile as I nodded in quick agreement, for of course my knowledge of Gretchen's breasts (and other parts) far surpassed Beano's. I also sensed that his friendship with the Furlong family was in some way connected to this interview.

"Let's visit the thumbsuckers," Beano said abruptly, and at once I realized that he was very busy. While we'd chatted, the telephones constantly rang, and hurrying young men put sheets of yellow paper into a wooden box on a corner of his desk. The box was quite full.

I followed him and now took note of the large, smoky, open room, in which rows of messy desks extended from wall to wall; placards revealed that groupings of these desks belonged to various departments—Sports, for example, and Metropolitan News. As telephones rang and people scurried (some yelled "Copy!"), it occurred to me that the *Telegram* was but a larger version of the *Buffalo Vindicator*. The clicks of thousands of typewriter keys made an unearthly sound.

At one end of this noisy, drafty place were large, smudged windows that looked down on Pennsylvania Avenue, and at the other was a yellow wall, stained brown by tobacco smoke, behind which a corridor led to a narrow staircase. Beano increased his pace as he led me up those stairs, two at a time, and into an annex: a conference room, accompanied by another row of offices. The first of these, with its door closed, belonged to Russell Morgan Beadle, the editor of the newspaper's opinion pages, and a moment later, Beano knocked. After perhaps thirty seconds, he knocked again, and the door was opened slowly, revealing an unfriendly, distracted expression that was attached to the face of Beadle.

"I've got no jurisdiction here, but I've got some influence," Beano said, and winked.

"This is the fellow I'm supposed to hire?" was the reply. Then Beadle shook his head, which was so hairless as to suggest, from certain angles, an alien planetoid. In the silence that followed, I thought how important luck is, and that mine came in the form of Gordon Gallatin—Beano. I also thought that the man I'd just met, possibly my new superior, seemed to harbor feelings that were unfriendly, and that was worrisome.

When I look back, I can see how my arrival—my original point of view, as well as my assertiveness—must have grated on Beadle. What is indisputable is that Beadle was desperately unhappy at that period of his life, and that relations between us would not have deteriorated so quickly if he had not been predisposed to hate me.

Matters took a bad turn almost at once, when he refused to publish one of my first pieces, a little commentary, entitled "Old Terrain," which mourned the closing of my former publication. I wrote this even though I'd not been invited to the farewell party—a slight, I confess, that still rankles. After all, most of Washington, or so I was told, showed up to toast Tobias and his dead magazine, and while some might have resented my good fortune at so quickly changing horses, I ought to have been included at the finale. Hubert Humphrey dropped by and praised the brave liberalism of the magazine, and so did Bobby Kennedy, who was witty and stayed for an hour. My neck grew red with envy when Madeleine Whitbridge told me later that she'd had an invigorating conversation about Vietnam with Dean Rusk.

She also told me that partygoers laughed long and hard at a joke about me and J. Edgar Hoover that I have forgotten, and that Gretchen (who, curiously, never mentioned it) had been among the revelers.

Despite my reservations about New Terrain's shrillness and its predictable politics, I had praised my comrades-in-arms for their perseverance in the face of death, and saluted them for a job well done. My piece, in short, reflected the feelings of someone who was proud to have been a part of a gallant enterprise and who, even as he moved on to better things, would never forget his debt. After Beadle refused to print it, I sulked for a few days, although I realized that such childish behavior gained me nothing.

Not long afterward, I heard from Esther, in a short note sent from New York, where she'd gone to find work. ("I'm not mad at you, Brandon," she wrote, "but you've been a bad boy. And you know what? I think you'll miss me much more than you can realize.") After that, I lost touch with Esther for a very long time. But I had odd dreams in which she played a part, and sometimes I would awaken with an unaccountable sadness that eluded my occasional attempts to explain it, but may explain why I held on to her little note.

*　*　*

Gretchen and I were married a few months later, in June of 1965, in an Episcopal ceremony officiated by an assistant to the Bishop of Washington. Almost everyone I'd gotten to know was there, under a tent at Lorton Hills, although Jacqueline Kennedy, whom I'd met but once, sent her regrets. Among those who showed up were Hubert Humphrey and Rusk, with whom I exchanged pleasantries, as well as ambassadors from Great Britain, France, and Portugal, along with several congressmen, including Bob Hudnut, who several times winked at me (to this day, I don't know who invited him), happy to be noticed by so many women, their exposed shoulders dewy and freckled. Beano of course was there, and many of Gretchen's classmates from Smith, but I was surprised to see Lionel Heftihed. (Later, Gretchen confessed that she'd once, briefly, been "involved" with Lionel; I felt an almost physical pain as I imagined their ancient intimacies.)

It was also a day filled with regrets. I wish, above all, that my parents had come, but I had persuaded the Furlongs that it was kinder not to invite them. My mother's condition had not improved, and I wanted to spare them the strain of a major social event far from home—or, for that matter, the strain of having to decide whether to attend such an event. I explained this in the note we sent afterward, along with a packet of photographs. I told them that they were missed and that I loved them very much. They did not, to my disappointment, respond, although they sent a wedding gift, a Crock-Pot, from Berger's. I had made a special point of inviting Chet Budge, but he did not bother to return his stiff little R.S.V.P. card.

I was sorry that I made Gretchen's father uncomfortable, but I was undoubtedly partly to blame. I have said that this will be an honest memoir, and, as I may have indicated, my sex drive is unusually strong. (I believe that one's sexual appetite corresponds in part to one's abilities in other fields.) It happened that on a Saturday morning, a few weeks before the wedding, Gretchen and I were in the stables, a quarter-mile from the main house; and the stallions pawing their hay and the smell of grass from the rolling hills had given urgency to my affection. "'Gather the rose of love, whilst yet is time,'" I murmured, quoting Spenser, while we stood outside an empty stall, the one next to Lucky Dog. In a trice, I persuaded Gretchen to remove her garments ("'Her gentle limbs did she undress,'" I went on, quoting Coleridge), and her whitened bare loins as well as my sizable, swollen parts might have been visible not only to Mr. Furlong but to Mrs. Furlong, who had preceded him. I noticed that Mr. Furlong wept silently as he walked his daughter, who wore her grandmother's wedding dress, to the makeshift altar.

Whenever I took a moment to assure both Furlongs that their daughter meant the world to me, neither looked enthusiastic, while Gretchen's brother, Preston, now and then squinted in a threatening manner. Perhaps they could see what I, being twenty-five, could not see for myself: how inexperienced we were, and how difficult it is to keep a promise when the promise involves the future.

We made a temporary home in my little place on P Street, the one that Esther had helped choose, and each morning I drove to work in my Pontiac coupe, a wedding gift from the Furlongs. I would stroll through the fourth-floor newsroom, which passed always in a blur, and make my way up the stairs to the alcove where the editorial page offices were situated. The four of us who worked there, I quickly realized, possessed individual strengths, but we were not a collegial group.

Along with myself and Beadle were two writers of modest ability: Morris Rosen and Jervis Tramm. Morris, whose speciality was nuclear weaponry, was close to the retirement age of sixty-eight, and it is quite possible that he knew more about these terrible weapons than any civilian alive. Morris rarely tackled other subjects and several times he became defiant when a piece was rejected; he would pound his desk while muttering phrases like "stupid cretin." I respected Morris, but knew at once that I would have problems with Jervis, a man of about thirty-five, who shared my interest in politics and diplomacy. Jervis lacked my heartland background, but he was, at that time, better versed in the ways of Washington, having covered Congress for more than nine years in a style that his peers generally regarded as plodding. All of this, I believe, would have worked itself out were it not for our supervisor.

The tone was set in the first week or so, when Beadle invited me to a breakfast in his office. My mood had been optimistic. I'd forgiven him for not running my little essay on *New Terrain;* after all, there were many other subjects. I had so looked forward to our meeting, and saw it as a chance, as I told Gretchen, to communicate basic principles. I remained in this hopeful humor for the few minutes that I sat alone in his lair, surrounded by the detritus (plaques, scrolls, banquet pictures, framed pages, an accordion of family photos) of thirty-odd years in the newspaper business.

"Let me tell you how things work in my little shop," Beadle said when he showed up five minutes after nine, saying this without a preliminary greeting or handshake.

"I'm anxious to hear," I said, with genuine enthusiasm, not realizing that I'd cut him off, and that this irritated him. When coffee and rolls were brought to us by our secretary, Marge Cavanaugh, a friendly and slightly overweight woman who was just crossing into the bitter territory of middle age, he seemed not to notice.

"We have a pretty simple routine," Beadle went on. "At nine sharp, the four of us meet in the conference room. I like to quickly decide what topics demand comment. Morris might have a nuclear worry—he's an expert. Jervis, as you ought to know, is perhaps the best-informed political writer in Washington"—I disagreed silently—"and I value his opinions highly." Beadle said some of this while his mouth was stuffed with a breakfast roll, and moist smacking sounds accompanied every sentence or so as he continued: "Sometimes, although it is very rare, I will disagree with Morris or Jervis, and we will argue. It works very well, or it has until now. You, Mr. Sladder, are something of a wild card, and I don't mean that in the best possible way."

I did not at first understand his meaning, and instead I looked at his head, its baldness so plain—the visible veins, the indentations at the temples, a reddish patch above an ear—that it made me uncomfortable, as if its innards were out. He had thick, distorting lenses, and his blue eyes were a blur.

"What I'm getting at, Mr. Sladder, is that I'm not entirely clear about your value to us. I gather that you fancy yourself something of an expert on the political scene, or perhaps the Cold War? But our little band's larder is well stocked with that sort of proficiency."

I nodded. Had he not, I wondered, read my work in *New Terrain*? Should I perhaps show him some of my best efforts from Buffalo? Was he, as I suddenly began to fear, deaf to my writer's voice? In the silence that followed, I knew that it was time for me to speak.

"I try to bring fresh insights and good reporting to every-thing I write," I said slowly. "That's why Beano brought me here. It is what I want to do."

Beadle took a large bite out of the remaining roll, which actually belonged to me. He was chewing when he took a gulp of his coffee and, somehow, choked on this mixture, so that the disgustingly lumpish result sprayed out onto his desk and papers.

"So it's all very simple," Beadle said, when he'd finished swallowing what he could and covered his desk with a sheet of newspaper. "We meet, we talk, we think, we write. I make the assignments, and I decide what is publishable." He paused, and wiped his glasses, and it seemed to me that his eyes were still out of focus. "I hope you realize that you're on probation here, Mr. Sladder, as anyone would be who starts in a new job. For your sake, I hope it works out."

I felt queasy. I wanted to ask Beadle what happened when we disagreed—did he force us to submit to his will? I worried in particular about Tramm, whose interests were in many cases mine. Jervis, I was soon to learn, had already gone behind my back and told others that I was an embar-rassment to the newspaper. His scheming was no doubt spurred by jealousy (he had read my work), but also, quite likely, by disagreements over America's growing involve-ment in Southeast Asia, which, as Lincoln would have put it, had begun to divide our smallish house.

* * *

I had seen Lyndon Johnson in crowds, but my first chance
to meet with him as an equal came in the fall of 1965,
when I'd been at my new job for about six months. Not to
mince words, my months at the newspaper had been hell-
ish; Beadle rejected most of what I wrote, and I sensed that
he wanted to fire me. When I attempted to comment on
changes in Soviet leadership, Beadle said that I had nothing
of value to add. When I sought to write about a poverty program, Jervis Tramm subtly undermined me. I sensed real
anger over our differences in foreign policy. Of course, I also
worried that L.B.J. did not grasp the nuances of regional
strife in Southeast Asia—that he did not have my urgent
sense that the fate of Vietnam was tied to the future of several other small, vital Oriental countries. But I was puzzled—and remain so—by people like Tramm and Beadle,

who seemed able to decide the largest moral questions with the snap of a finger. During our morning meetings, I would propose a topic and get only silence in reply.

Although Beadle and Tramm were aligned against me (Morris Rosen seemed indifferent), I never thought of going behind anyone's back. What happened was simply this: During a three-day interval in October, when Beadle and Tramm were attending a governors' conference in Virginia, I decided to jot down a few thoughts and substitute those for the boilerplate that Tramm had left behind. Morris's objection was sound enough; he pointed out that Beadle always insisted on approving whatever we ran. But his argument was not persuasive; and so we published an eloquent little piece, entirely in my voice, in which, while urging restraint, I praised L.B.J. for a brave civil rights policy and also inserted a few words of prudent advice about his international ambitions, while not actually taking him to task.

The next day, the White House called to ask who had penned those words, which had given the President such pleasure. To my astonishment, I was invited to meet him face-to-face—an invitation I accepted at once. I remember how Tramm and Beadle, when they returned from Richmond, regarded me with an envy and mistrust that seemed to border on revulsion. Beadle called me into his office, where we sat for some minutes, but he was unable to speak; I tried not to stare at the pulsating indentations of his skull. Rather than praise me for my work, he said, finally, "You sneaky little bastard. If it weren't for Beano, I'd make sure you never worked in this business again." I was discouraged by his outburst.

*　*　*

I freely admit that it meant a lot to me actually to sit, à deux, inside the Oval Office, and I stole glances at the paintings and little mementos, including a Remington horse and cowboy hat hung alongside a pair of antlers that once had been attached to the head of a Texas buck. When Johnson saw me peeking out the window, from which we could see the mansion's sunny grounds and the Monument, he put his freckled hand on my shoulder and said, "It's something, son." I told him how pleased I had been that Hubert had come to my wedding, and how kindly Deputy Secretary X had spoken of him. Within minutes, it was as if we had known one another for years.

The President was interested in my thoughts on a number of issues, including equal rights for people of African heritage, but he seemed to pay closest attention when he leaned toward me, his large head filling up the space before my eyes. "Why does Beadle want to hurt me in Vietnam?" he asked, with a pitiful whine. "Why can't he see that all we're trying to do is help those little people?" Later he asked, "Who is Beadle fucking? Can he get that little pecker up?"

I quickly understood why Johnson had summoned me. From my few kind, anonymous words, he had come to view me as a friend; or a sympathetic ear. Of Beadle's personal life, I assured him, I knew nothing, and had no real reason to doubt his commitment to heterosexuality. I also shared my thought that critics were too quick to dismiss his policy in Southeast Asia (words I have regretted) and repeated myself because he looked so grateful. I saw him then in all his flawed grandeur, and realized, as Schopenhauer wrote, that "if you stroke a cat, it will purr; and as inevitably, if you praise a man, a sweet expression of delight will appear on his face." L.B.J. appeared to delight in my company, but, as our conversation was winding down, something odd occurred, something that I set down only hesitantly, but out of a duty to history: The President unzipped his fly and, I'm quite sure, drew forth—I looked away, so I cannot swear to it—his organ.

"Brandon, tell me: What is Charles de Gaulle against this?" I was, to say the least, flabbergasted.

"I cannot say, sir," I managed at length, in some embarrassment.

"Brandon, let me tell you: He doesn't measure up. Neither does Ho Chi Minh." He shook his head and looked at me with woeful eyes that reminded me of horses that pawed the ground at Lorton Hills.

I wondered again why he had summoned me, for I was, at that point in my career, relatively obscure.

"Get your notebook out, son," the President then said, and as he continued to pace (his energy was boundless), I saw, to my relief, that he was zipped up. Then he stood at my side, his large hand falling once more to my shoulder, and said, "I am going to do what your President thinks he has to do to protect American interests." I wrote with furious haste. "I am not going to be the President who cut and ran when the going got tough. This President will never let you down."

He paused and looked as if he had just finished a cigarette, exhaling with pleasure. I took that moment to seek his views on relations with Europe, on his hopes for our impoverished citizenry, but he shook his head and gave me a tolerant smile. Then he said, "I want you to tell Beano how much I admire him and his newspaper. And I want you to tell people there to give me a fair shake."

Moments later, a young Marine helped me find my way to a door, and from there to the Pennsylvania Avenue gate. I looked back at the whitewashed mansion and realized, almost dizzily, that I was in possession of news. My heart beat with a wild thump-thump, and it pounded that way until I returned to the office and wrote about my exclusive interview with all the speed and joy of a police reporter covering his first major crime.

After my tête-à-tête with Johnson, I got a prized back-pat from Beano, who stopped me to say, "A goddam scoop!" My reply was modest—"Just fucking good luck!"—but for the first time, colleagues on the fourth floor took notice. Among them was Aileen Frugtsaft, a woman in her mid-twenties, whose lively prose set her apart. Aileen's beat was science and medicine, but, like myself, she was absorbed by the events of our time. A few days after my story appeared, she called out as I passed her gray metal desk, which was covered by multicolored copy paper and inky proofs.

When I alluded to my good luck, she said, "People make their own luck," and, I recall, stared at me with unwavering intensity.

"Maybe so, but then it's not really luck, is it?" I replied, enjoying our intellectual banter as our eyes locked.

"I also believe that smart people are luckier than dumb people," she insisted, unblinking.

Aileen was curiously insecure about her work, and often asked people at nearby desks to read whatever she'd strung together. Now she asked me to look at an article she'd begun about a new strain of influenza that was expected to arrive in California. I'd noticed that she wore a loose blouse, and as I bent to read, I wondered whether she knowingly permitted me to glimpse the tiny pink nipple that completed the pale droop of an ample breast.

"I wish you'd tell Beano that I want to cover the White House," she whispered, breathing these words with a warm puff as I read about this immigrant virus. "Would you?" Aileen said, for I had been distracted and had not answered the first time.

"I do not think he would listen to me," I said, and sensed her displeasure when she stiffened. "But," I hastily added, for it has always been my rule to help, whenever possible, talented coworkers, "I shall try," at which she relaxed and smiled, blinking, as I moved on, with a wave.

I had hoped that Gretchen would be just as enthusiastic about my story, but she actually said, "I wish you'd quit strutting about," and seemed to take no pleasure that my name was becoming known. She seemed, rather, to harbor an odd sort of jealousy, as if my personal triumphs somehow excluded her. I sensed a particular sourness in her mood as the holiday season intruded; and during Thanksgiving Day, which we celebrated at Lorton Hills, I felt as if the entire

Furlong clan had somehow reexamined me and found me wanting. At one point, her brother, Preston, spilled cranberry sauce into my lap and did not apologize. Later, he whispered, "What are you doing to make my little sister so miserable?" I had no idea what he was talking about, and visibly shrugged.

I know that I ought to have been more attentive to Gretchen, such as when I learned, in the spring of 1966, that she was pregnant (it must have happened around Christmas). But it would have been irresponsible of me to stay home when I had been invited to attend briefings at the State Department, or share an off-the-record dinner with Bob McNamara and a dozen important journalists. My editorial page colleagues, who began to seem increasingly provincial, were suspicious ("Suspicion," Shakespeare pointed out, "always haunts the guilty mind"), and I was certain that Beadle and Tramm, more than ever, did not wish me well. In short, I had a lot on my plate, but Gretchen was unsympathetic.

As Gretchen became more pregnant, we knew that the P Street apartment would be too small, and her parents helped us to buy a small house on O Street, west of Wisconsin Avenue. Like all young marrieds, we set about making it our own, filling it with the knickknacks that encapsulate a life: snapshots from our wedding (in the background was my friend Bob Hudnut); a blanket chest that had belonged to Gretchen's great-great-grandmother, and was made by hand in Philadelphia; the official White House photograph of myself with Lyndon Johnson; a Kermanshah rug from Lorton Hills that now filled our living room with an orange glow; and most precious: a photograph taken of me with Jack Kennedy at Lorton Hills (Gretchen is standing between us), framed in walnut and mounted alongside a shiny brass PT-109 tie clasp that the martyred President had given to our family. The glossy, almost phosphorescent print (we all look toothily amused) was inscribed in blue ink, "With thanks for a pleasant evening, John F. Kennedy." It rested on the mantel over a fireplace; it reminded me how grateful I was to have known him.

When Brandon—Branny—was born in the fall of 1966, at Sibley (eight pounds, one ounce), it was a time of great happiness; tears sprang to my eyes whenever I saw the infant's cherub face and tickled his pink toes. Returning from work, with Branny flailing about, his face filled with love, completed what certainly ought to have been a perfect time in our lives. So it was even more difficult to understand why Gretchen's eyes were so red so often.

It was Madeleine Whitbridge—acting, I'm sure, out of kindness—who first warned me that Gretchen was less happy than I'd imagined. Several weeks after Branny was born, she called and suggested that we meet for lunch at Sans Souci, on Seventeenth Street, not far from the White House. I appreciated, as always, her delicate tact.

Madeleine got there first, and was seated at a table toward the rear, wearing her trademark large silver necklace. I had rapidly walked the ten blocks from the newspaper, and a light film of perspiration had seeped into my wool suit. I went hastily to her table, leaned to kiss her powdered cheek, and raised my hand to signal a waiter that we were ready.

"And how is Branny?" she asked, patting my hand. "You must have pictures."

I was embarrassed that I did not, and it struck me that I'd fallen ever so slightly in Madeleine's estimation for not being able to produce them. It was the last time I was to be pictureless.

"I remember when Willy and I were first married, and we had Ariadne, and how much joy she gave us," Madeleine said with a sad expression. "Willy, as you know, was always away and I found myself alone with her, sometimes for weeks at a time."

It was rare that Madeleine talked, even fleetingly, about her husband, the O.S.S. veteran of derring-do. I had recently come to doubt that Willy Whitbridge's fatal mishap in the Tidal Basin was an accident, but I still did not know her well enough to ask if she shared my suspicions. I realized that Madeleine had not previously mentioned a daughter.

"It must have been nice, those weeks alone with Ariadne," I said.

"Of course it wasn't," she replied, with some sharpness. "But those were different times. We had a war to fight." Two glasses of Chardonnay arrived, and as we raised and clinked them, she added, "Today, I would resent it. That is how Gretchen feels, or so I believe."

We stared at one another. Had Gretchen confided in Madeleine, or was this an example of the gossip that infects our town? "Do you believe this, Madeleine, or do you *know* this?" I asked, my voice no longer so cordial.

She shook her head solemnly. "It is something I know," she said softly.

Both of us then studied the menus, and Madeleine licked her thin lips when a platter of *coquilles St. Jacques* or a steaming bowl of onion soup passed by. The salad, moist and green with sprigs of red and amber peppers, tempted us both, and so for that matter did the pygmy filets mignons on toast. I urged her to order without restraint, as I was enjoying my first experience with an expense account.

"You must appreciate the difficulties that face Gretchen," Madeleine said at once, with sternness. "She has given up her freedom, in many ways her family, to be with you. But how often are you with her?"

I did not know how to reply. Madeleine could have no knowledge of our very personal moments, or our sexual passion. How could I talk about the pleasure it gave me, at the age of twenty-seven, to watch my son attempt to master the rudiments of human behavior? I recall perfectly that moment of silence, for our salads arrived and, simultaneously, Madeleine told me something that nearly shattered my composure.

"I have it on good authority that Lionel Heftihed sometimes visits your house," she said, lifting a fork filled with greenery and placing it at the entrance to her small mouth. My heart pounded.

I had lost track of Lionel, apart from his appearance at our wedding, where we did not have a moment to catch up. I'd heard that he had moved to New York, and returned to Washington now and again in some journalistic capacity. Within the past month or so, he had published a short biography of Henry Adams, and was fortunate enough to have had it reviewed kindly by the *New York Times*, as well as by a few small magazines where he maintained friendships. Sometimes it still haunted me that he once had been intimate with Gretchen (and Gretchen, I suppose, with Lionel), but my impression had been that they no longer had any substantive connection.

"I was not aware that he was living here," I said.

Madeleine shook her head, pausing while she chewed her crisp salad. *"Au contraire, mon vieux,"* she said with a diminished smile. "We gave him a marvelous party last month when his wonderful book was published, and in his toast, he looked around and said that he had never imagined that he had so many friends in one place."

I knew that Madeleine must occasionally entertain without including me in her plans, but it wounded me that she had sponsored an event for a former colleague and had not numbered me among the guests. I knew precisely who would have attended, and certainly had no regrets at having missed the party; but the point, really, was to have been asked. (My heart froze: Had not Gretchen dashed out for a few hours one late afternoon, not telling me where?) As the waiter removed her salad, at least half of it remaining, Madeleine seemed to realize that she had rattled me.

"Poor dear," she said, and reached across the table to pat the top of my hand. "I am not telling you these things in order to upset you. I am telling you these things because I care so much about you and Gretchen. And, believe me, I have an unerring sense of when a marriage appears to be progressing on the wrong foot."

The truth was that I hadn't been entirely honest, for I'd begun to notice in Gretchen a total indifference to my career; often, as when I told her of my wish to write a syndicated column, she looked at me with an expression that I can only describe as pained. I had long come to appreciate that Gretchen had more limitations than those I've already catalogued; she had never, for instance, been very interested in the sweep of history. For her, there was more pleasure in mounting a horse than in having a conversation with McGeorge Bundy, and in the months of our courtship, these differences had not seemed important. Yet she had recently arrived at a new and disturbingly naive political awareness. Just the other day, carrying tiny Branny, she had joined a crowd in Lafayette Park and protested America's military involvement in Vietnam. She did this despite my having told her that I found such mob behavior to be simpleminded, and urged her to find other causes. All these conflicting recollections struck me as I sat with Madeleine at Sans Souci. Her slightly discolored hand had continued to pat mine even as our main courses arrived (she had the filets mignons on toast, and I the scallops) and her expression had become more solicitous.

"Gretchen and I love one another," I said, and now confessed, "But we have found ourselves, now and then, on opposite sides of the ocean."

Madeleine looked puzzled, then nodded patiently. "If so, how could you even see one another—an ocean, after all, is so vast?"

I shook my head, and smiled wanly, wondering if Madeleine was presenting me with a parable. But I could not forget what she had told me moments before, and as I speared a scallop, I said, "I cannot believe that she has any lingering interest in Lionel."

"I believe that he is the one who long ago dropped Gretchen," said Madeleine. "I know that Gretchen, above all, admires accomplished men. As do we all. And now she is politically involved, as Lionel once wished her to be."

My face reddened, and I vowed to spend more time at home, perhaps to accompany Gretchen to one of the antique stores that are so temptingly a part of the Virginia countryside—to make our next Thanksgiving worthy of its name. I also had an uncontrollable urge to stop by O Street, to see that all was well with Gretchen and Branny, and that they were alone.

*   *   *

My newspaper was owned by the last progeny of the Von Helsing family, a brother and sister in their late sixties with a reputation for dissolution. I cannot claim that I knew them well—or even that I knew them—but I remember speaking to the siblings at a garden party in Cleveland Park, in the spring of 1967. Both had pink skin and long, thin necks and exceedingly roomy collars; they barely moved their lips when they talked. I greeted them warmly and, in the course of our brief conversation, discovered that the three of us shared similar views about the President.

In a new century, it is difficult to explain Vietnam and the rupture in civility that marked that time ("The center cannot hold," I wrote more than once). Today I regret having called Lionel Heftihed a "cowardly traitor" because he wanted no part of an Asian war, and hope that he regrets calling me a "bloodthirsty shit" because, despite my tormented qualms, I supported my native land. Then, however, even my wife questioned my motives, and when I tried to explain that I had doubts, too, it was as if Gretchen had gone deaf; she refused to follow my reasoned arguments. (I have always wondered how the infantile Branny was affected by our discussions, which would sometimes culminate with Gretchen's hysteria. Once she threw a Furlong heirloom at me, a plate that passed through a bowed glass window and onto O Street and shattered my equilibrium.)

Through the summer and fall of 1967, our editorial meetings became, if that is possible, more unbearable. Our little conference room was airless, and one felt oppressed by photographic portraits of deceased, hairy-faced editors that decorated the yellow walls. Sometimes, the others would chat contentedly, as if I were not there; were I to mention something I'd learned from one of the many high officials who had begun to confide in me, Beadle would shake his shiny, concave skull, pityingly. Only Morris Rosen appeared to pay attention. "Ask about the military budget, don't forget," he would say, and I promised Morris that I would, patting his arm. Then I'd fall silent beneath the watchful eyes and scraggly beards of the dead editors along the wall.

Above all, I was finding it increasingly hard to associate myself with the group's lazy prose and predictable thinking, made worse because Beadle continued to block me from publishing my serious thoughts. He seemed to take sadistic pleasure in forcing me to concentrate on matters that held little interest for me—teachers' pay, perhaps, or faraway events (an Indian earthquake)—and after a while, the meetings were so numbing that I skipped one, then another. When no one objected, I stayed away regularly, and for the first time I thought about resigning. No doubt I would have left the paper were it not for my new family responsibilities.

One morning, I went to a bracing session on Vietnam in the Old Executive Office Building, a discussion that touched on secret plans that could lead to many deaths. I was honored to be included (no Beadle, no Tramm), and listened carefully to the men, some in uniform, at the dark table. I sat on a folding chair close to the wall, and at one point, I leaned toward an important military source and, sotto voce, said, "It sounds as if you still believe there is light at the end of that tunnel." The veteran produced a weary smile and said, "All I know is that I have to keep digging in order to find out."

Afterward, I wrote down this little exchange, for his words excited me. I certainly didn't endorse the sentiment; I tried only to interpret it, because—I repeat myself—I was always deeply ambivalent about the war. In any event, I had an almost physical need to write about it, and one late afternoon in the winter of 1967 (humming a tune from the brand-new *Sgt. Pepper* album), I gave in to my needs with a rush of pleasure. When I was done, I offered the eight-hundred-word result to Beadle; with foolish hope, I suggested that he simply print it as a signed column—so that the responsibility would be mine alone.

"But I think what you've written is drivel, Sladder," Beadle said, with apparent distaste.

"What do you mean?" I asked.

"I mean poppycock, bunkum, piffle, bilge," he replied, his eyes blurring.

"I respectfully disagree," I replied, with disbelief, fighting to gain control.

Beadle shook his head. "Then that's how our conversation ends," he said, though it didn't end there.

It is hard to say with exactitude what happened next. No doubt, both Von Helsings liked what I'd written, and appreciated my courtesy in showing them a copy (I now and then sent them little notes), but I don't know whether they, or an intermediary, actually approached Beadle. Possibly they, like me, saw that Beadle's refusal to welcome contrary opinions was a serious weakness; and in any case it was hard to miss the outward signs of his personal disintegration. After my little column appeared, Beadle would spew out obscenities, uncontrollably, whenever we passed one another, and once I saw his devoted secretary, Marge Cavanaugh, weeping. (When I tried to comfort her, she brushed away my hand.) Jervis Tramm called me a "shill" for the government, and, luckily for him, the fist that I aimed at his mouth was blocked by Morris Rosen. When I attempted to explain privately to Beadle that I was lucky to be on good terms with the White House, the State Department, the Pentagon, and the Central Intelligence Agency, and that there was value in being able to analyze the arguments that preceded every major decision, he regarded me with unfocused detestation.

Beadle's decision to resign was an utter surprise, and I never quite understood his motives, although after so many years at the helm, it is clear that he needed new challenges. In a farewell column, he quoted Emerson—"We countenance each other in this life of show, puffing, advertisement, and manufacture of public opinion; and excellence is lost sight of in the hunger for sudden performance and praise"—but did not bother to add a formal good-bye. He could not know that in many ways, I deeply admired him.

As it happened, Beadle's unhappy leave-taking coincided with good news: Within a few months, I was going to be given my own column. It was Beano who told me, and when he asked how I felt about that, I replied, "That makes me so fucking happy." I recall that Beano seemed distracted, and that he asked me, apropos of nothing, how well I knew the Von Helsings and how often I'd sent short notes to them.

"They're a strange pair, even when they're sober," Beano said, and did not appear to believe me when I told him that we'd barely met. He shook his head, and said, "You're a strange one, too, Brandon," which I took as a compliment. But after that, I sensed a coolness from Beano, which saddened and perplexed me.

*   *   *

People born in an age of television may not understand what it meant to get a column of one's own, but that was my good fortune in the spring of 1968. From the start, I felt the keenest of pleasures. It was as if I'd been starving, and strawberry shortcake, covered by warm chocolate, was served up; or as if I'd not been able to gratify myself and a woman with creamy skin and wondrous breasts, her sweet, hot limbs parted, lay eagerly beside me.

At first, my column was bought by four newspapers; then, within weeks, a dozen, then (at about the time President Johnson decided not to run again) thirty. Someone called me a "new, urgent mind," and another saw "uncommon eloquence and wit." I was grateful for these encomia (which I quote for the sake of context), but never forgot that Washington is a city of flatterers. I especially valued

123

the encouragement of friends, such as Aileen Frugtsaft, the talented science reporter, who said that I was redefining the art of the political column. Although I tended to walk quickly through the newsroom, darkly radiant and populated at all hours by weary, unshaven men and unkempt women, I found that a stop by Aileen's overflowing desk was reassuring. I sometimes accompanied her to Pica's Roost, a neighborhood pub, where we talked happily about the issues that stimulated our minds.

Aileen once said, humorously, that my column was a jinx, pointing out the terrible things that immediately followed its debut. In truth, both of us were deeply affected by the murder in April of Martin Luther King, Jr. (I described the subsequent riots as "a tragedy unleavened by hope"), and, in June, of Robert Kennedy, whom I knew slightly (and may have underrated), by which time forty-five newspapers were running my column. On the night of the day that Kennedy died, I went with Aileen to Pica's Roost, and both of us wept, despite my personal support for Hubert. I comforted her as she comforted me, our bodies barely touching, and while that did not remove the sense of loss, for us and for the nation, it lessened it somewhat.

I had hoped for some sign of approval from my former colleagues, especially Jervis, and at the very least expected more collegiality after Beadle retired. But they kept to themselves, and sometimes laughed uncontrollably, not including me in their badinage. I suppose that their laughter was release from the pressure of work, for they were somewhat shorthanded; the Von Helsings had not hired a replacement for Beadle and, of course, I had my column to tend to. No doubt they (as well as the sadly unfulfilled Marge Cavanaugh) resented my move into Beadle's office, and my habit of thinking and writing with the door shut. I was sympathetic, and my hand of friendship remained extended.

Gretchen, as I have hinted, was rarely in sympathy with my views. For instance, she had supported the chimerical candidacies of Eugene McCarthy and Bobby Kennedy, while I saw Hubert, who had attended our wedding three years before, as a family friend. She was undoubtedly egged on by Lionel Heftihed, whose angry words popped up in what seemed like dozens of small, smudgy magazines.

At the time that Lionel reentered our lives, he was close to forty; his towering hair had begun to gray, and he'd put on weight. But he had not lost his self-importance or his dilettantism; one moment he was holding forth on the Mexican economy, and then he dined out on his overly praised book, *Henry Adams's Education and Mine*. I did not mind his quick-change talents, but I did object to his proselytizing in behalf of retreat from Vietnam, especially when it affected my family's tranquillity.

In the summer of 1968, Lionel encouraged Gretchen to become even more involved in his "antiwar" activities, and almost persuaded her to accompany him on a self-indulgent excursion to Chicago (I put my foot down) for the Democratic Convention. Quoting Lincoln, I wrote that, like bad relief pitchers, some people find that "it is impossible to foresee all the incidents which may attend and all the ruin

Final

which may follow." Gretchen pretended not to see the point when I thrust that column before her during breakfast. She even brushed it away. Her outlook baffled me; seldom has our nation been so divided, and yet she stubbornly took refuge in cheap slogans. As that agitated summer wore on (by the end of it, Dick Nixon and Spiro Agnew were facing Hubert and Edmund Muskie), Gretchen seemed increasingly distracted, and her outbursts became less controllable.

Gretchen and Aileen Frugtsaft met one another for the first time at a newsroom reception in honor of Morris Rosen's fortieth anniversary at the newspaper. A papier-mâché nuclear missile dangled from the ceiling, blackened by dead moths and brightened by rows of fluorescent tubes, and along its side were the words: "Morris: A Ten-Megaton Colleague!" Cheese cubes and soft drinks were heaped upon metal desks, and just about everyone was there, from Beano to the copyboys—even the Von Helsings, although not, notably, Russell Morgan Beadle, who had moved to New Hampshire or, perhaps, Maine, and intended to stay put. I did not know everyone by name, but I enjoyed the speeches and the bonhomie; and I was thrilled when the Von Helsings took me aside and told me how pleased they were by my column, then only six months old. Both siblings, I thought, looked sickly, and all of us were aware of rumors that they might sell or close the newspaper, but they stayed for nearly an hour.

It ought to have been a cheery evening among peers, but the age would not allow it; my stomach hurt when

Gretchen, who had been talking to Beano, saw me sharing a laugh with Aileen and came to join us. I introduced her to my coworker, but was embarrassed for them both—slender Gretchen, her blond curls a little damp, and the more womanly Aileen, her darker features insightful. Gretchen asked, "Are you a reporter, Aileen?" and Aileen said, "I guess you don't read your husband's newspaper." Moments later, Gretchen whispered, "I suppose she's a charter member of your fan club," and her sarcasm made me genuinely sad.

"More than seventy newspapers buy my column," I said.

"You are a young, fresh, witty voice," Gretchen replied, this time loudly enough for others to sense tension between us.

Yet my basic feelings for Gretchen were intact. When little Branny crawled onto our bed on a Sunday morning, I was filled with happiness; I loved to swing him over my head, listening to his breathless, little-boy laughter. If the physical side of our marriage had become less important to Gretchen, I believed that would change. If difficult times lay ahead for the Sladders and the nation, it was not yet obvious to me.

* * *

As my column became more popular, so did I, and I found myself being drawn deeper into the social life of Washington. All at once, I knew everyone (occasionally I even sensed a small stir when I entered a room), and my chief regret was that Gretchen seemed unable to share my success. I suppose that is why I urged her to host a dinner party of her own; and so, on an extraordinarily humid night in September of 1968, we celebrated my twenty-ninth birthday. Gretchen had been reluctant at first, but we invited an interesting group with every hope that the hours would sparkle.

We had asked Madeleine Whitbridge and Jasper Munroe; Beano and his wife, Samantha; the Swiss ambassador, a man of great charm and sophistication; Ed Muskie, who was in town despite his busy schedule as Hubert's running mate, and Ed's wife, Jane. That seemed to me a splendid group, although we needed an extra woman, because the Swiss ambassador's wife was in Bern. I suggested Aileen Frugtsaft, because of her mounting interest in domestic policy. In that case, Gretchen replied, she wanted Lionel Heftihed, and when I saw that she was indifferent to my strong feelings, I agreed. I'd wanted to ask Bob Hudnut, but my old friend was campaigning for an open Senate seat in Missouri.

It should be obvious that such an occasion was of great value to my budding column. Jasper Munroe was always interesting—he knew the Senate as well as any man; the Switzerlander usually had a few international insights. And of course Ed Muskie (I knew him less well, having met him once or twice) might give me a nugget from the thick of the campaign. I had hoped that Ed and Jane would get there before the others, so that we could talk privately and openly, and I saw it as a bad omen when Lionel was the first to arrive. I tried to greet him warmly, for we'd not actually talked to one another for a few years, but I detected something furtive in his expression as he tossed his graying hair; his visage had become, if anything, more supercilious. Fortunately, Madeleine and Jasper came soon afterward and the five of us fell into an animated conversation about the humidity.

It was a pity that our air-conditioning wasn't working well, and Jasper's light gray suit, already damp when he sat down, was quickly soaked through. Moisture also streaked Madeleine's face, making clefts in her chalky makeup. Lionel's once-splendid head of hair became straggly and, I noticed, separated at the crown to reveal an incipient bald spot that he kept touching.

The heat steadily became more intense, prompting someone—Jasper, I think—to remark upon nature's deceptive trick when boiling frogs alive. Hotness leaked from the kitchen, where coq au vin was being prepared, and our male servant, Luis, whom we'd borrowed from Gretchen's parents, excreted wetness onto the glasses of chilled white wine that he distributed. Gretchen, who wore a short yellow dress and at that point managed to look dry, urged the men to remove their ties and jackets; but even that admonition seemed pointless by the time the Gordon Gallatins—Beano and Samantha—arrived. Samantha, who had a distant, fixed expression, wore a pale pink dress that quickly turned dark red beneath her armpits; Beano himself looked exhausted and, I thought for the first time, old. Aileen Frugtsaft, who appeared not long after Beano, had prepared for the weather by wearing a thin blouse that was rather loose and low cut. I could intuit that Gretchen judged her to be vulgar, and it is true that one could not help noticing Aileen's emphatic, freckled breasts.

I had an intimation that the evening might not turn out well when the Swiss diplomat, who was just as uncomfortable as the rest of us, refused to remove his jacket, at which point I sensed that Gretchen was close to tears. Both of us were also worried about the Muskies, who had not yet shown up; and, with the silent gestures of a married couple, we wondered if perhaps the senator had forgotten his obligation. The Muskies' absence would have been a particular humiliation, because we'd let everyone know that they'd be there, and my suspicion was that Ed was something of a "draw" on this hot night. The others, however, tried to carry on with gallantry, as if the party were complete, and I remember the conversation as if it had taken place last night.

"It has been such a ghastly time," Madeleine said, speaking for all of us. "Assassination, riot, a sense of anarchy."

"The center cannot hold, it seems," said the Swiss ambassador, with a shrewd look, first at me and then at a few others.

"You feel awful, because you feel that nothing is going to get better," said Aileen, with a shrug that set off freckly tremors along her bosom.

"I'll tell you, Lyndon is glad to head back to the ranch," said Jasper Munroe.

"The poor man must be so relieved to get away," said Madeleine, as if she hadn't heard Jasper.

I heard Lionel emit a sneering laugh that I'd come to recognize long ago, in the corridor of *New Terrain*.

"He can run, but he can't hide," said Lionel, patting his matted hair.

"You all should read Lionel's wonderful book about Henry Adams," Madeleine offered, with a sweet smile.

Just as one or two guests began to discuss Lionel's little biography, purporting to have read it, we heard sirens. It is always a little thrilling to see Secret Service men standing about one's house, and when we went to the windows, we saw several of them, dressed darkly, their faces drenched. Gretchen and I were so pleased that Ed and Jane had managed to get to O Street, despite the demands of a presidential campaign, and when we talked about it later, we decided that we could not blame the Maine senator for anything that went wrong. In fact, no one was more at ease than Ed Muskie, who instantly made a joke about the temperature—here and on the campaign trail. I liked Ed for his self-deprecating humor and his integrity (I never witnessed his famous temper), and was proud to number him among my friends. Jane, too.

But after Ed and Jane arrived, the talk quickly turned to politics, and voices began to rise in excitement—then, unhappily, in anger. I'll confess to a lifetime habit of listening to other conversations as I carry on my own, and I was pleased to see how Madeleine and Samantha embraced Gretchen and complimented her on our house and its furnishings, stopping, I noticed, to admire, as I sometimes did, the personally inscribed photograph from Jack Kennedy. But I did not like it when I heard Lionel holding forth on the election with curious snorts of smug laughter, or when the Swiss diplomat interrupted to ask, with oozing sympathy, how a great country like the United States had ended with such a shabby choice—Nixon and Humphrey. I looked whenever possible at Muskie, to see if any of this upset him, but Ed's long and turtlelike face rarely gave anything away, and he appeared to be enjoying himself with Jasper, his former Senate colleague. I saw that the Swiss fellow, sweating terribly, had just discovered Aileen, and that whenever Aileen leaned forward to gobble up some of the cashew nuts that we had placed here and there, he leaned, too, as if transfixed by her cleavage and its pinkish denouement.

The truth is that I blame no one but Lionel. What I remember was bending down to whisper something or other in

Aileen's ear (I cannot remember what) and then looking up to see Lionel, his lips vibrating with incoherent rage. "I will not vote for this man or for his Humphrey lackey!" Lionel said in a loud, triumphant voice, his finger pointing at Muskie, who looked over his shoulder, as if Lionel must have meant someone else.

I had been waiting for Lionel to lose his fragile temper and turned to him. "Then you will have Richard Nixon, and you will still have your damned war!" I rejoined, nodding at Ed, although in truth Nixon did not frighten me as he did others.

Lionel turned quite red and his hair flew about.

"My damned war? *You* are the fucking mouthpiece of this murdering government, and everyone here knows it."

Aileen leapt from our sofa. "I know of no one who has more integrity than Brandon," she said, words for which I will always be grateful.

At that point, eyes turned toward Muskie, then me. Ed looked at Jane as if to convey a signal of some sort. Gretchen, who did not rise to my defense, then said, "Please please please please *please!* No fighting!" She blinked as if to beat back an invasion of tears.

"We haven't even had our first course," Madeleine said after a few seconds of utter silence, and then laughed nervously as a salty rivulet made its way through her makeup. "It smells so good, Gretchen!" she added, to put my wife at ease.

"It *is* awfully damn hot," said Beano, with a laugh much like Madeleine's as Samantha, sitting rigidly, seemed to shudder.

"In every sense," I said, with a calming smile.

I moved closer to Muskie, sensing that he might wish to leave at any moment and not forgetting my obligations as a columnist. "How do you rate your chances?" I asked.

"Hubert's starting to act like himself, so I'd say I'm cautiously optimistic," said the senator, patting my knee as he shared this confidence.

I looked up and observed Lionel glaring at us as I made a mental note, and then saw Gretchen smiling patiently at Lionel. For a moment, I felt like an outsider to our marriage, as well as to my country. I thought of something that Lippmann had written forty years before: "For the modern man who has ceased to believe, without ceasing to be credulous, hangs, as it were, between heaven and earth, and is at rest nowhere." I wish that I'd had the presence of mind to quote it.

Luis had worked for years for the Furlongs, and we were glad to have him for the evening. But he was not a careful servant, and he seemed unaware that globules were falling from his face into the platters of coq au vin and the *haricots verts* and miniature parsleyed potatoes that accompanied it. Others at our table did, however, appear to notice these things, and I saw that Beano's wife refused to eat; so did the Swiss ambassador, who made a charming excuse about his girth. The temperature in our dining room had by now surpassed one hundred and five degrees, and I could see that Gretchen was afraid that our guests were miserable. My concern was not their discomfort, which was intense, but the likelihood of another explosion from Lionel, who fidgeted between bites and kept looking angrily at Muskie and me. I worried that he would upset Ed, but Muskie seemed indifferent to anything but the temperature, which affected his appetite, too. I tried to lighten the mood, and asked if anyone had seen any good movies, but Lionel said that his neighborhood theater had burned down in the spring riots.

In the middle of the main course, the telephone rang, as it had several times earlier. Luis took the call as he had the others, but this time he approached the table and, in his approximation of English, driplets dropping, told me that the White House was on the line. Others regarded me with interest as I went to the hallway.

It was not unusual to hear from the White House; most often it was a functionary in the press office, who would alert me to a briefing. This time, however, I was astounded to hear the voice of the President himself, the first time L.B.J. had ever called me. I was short of breath, but also humbled; after all, at the age of precisely twenty-nine, I was actually talking to the President while two United States senators, a newspaper editor, and others sat at my table. Johnson, as you may have guessed, wanted to tell me something of immense importance: he was inclined to announce a halt in the bombing of North Vietnam, but wanted to talk to a few influential people beforehand to seek their thoughts—people like myself. What did I think?

"I believe it is a good decision," I said in a low voice.

"Will it help Hubert?" he asked.

I said that I thought so. I don't know if he realized that Ed Muskie was there. I itched to tell him.

"Am I doing the right thing?" he asked in a plaintive voice, almost a wail. I pitied him as I debated with myself the rightness of offering comfort.

As we spoke, Gretchen came into the hall and looked at me quizzically. I waved my hand and mouthed the word "Lyn-don," whereupon she looked alarmed, and her eyes blinked like semaphores, signaling the tears that lay just ahead. Then she tugged at my arm, as if returning to the table mattered more than discussing the most urgent question of our time. I saw that Gretchen was now as soaked with perspiration as the rest of us. I also sensed that she was very, very angry.

"I want to tell you a few ideas about ending that damned war for good," Johnson said, but as he started, Gretchen pulled at me with her powerful arms, as well-muscled as her horsewoman's legs.

I could not stop what happened next: Gretchen was bending down to the telephone outlet and, while I succeeded in pushing her away as she yanked at the cord, she was clearly unimpressed by my caller and, furthermore, was determined to end our conversation by any means.

"Mr. President, we are having an emergency," I said. "God bless you in your quest!" I managed to add, as Gretchen, with a surprising burst of strength, wrenched the receiver from my hand and slammed it into its black cradle.

Now it was my turn to be angry. Did Gretchen understand that her precipitate action could very well affect the future of our country and the lives of thousands of American servicemen? She looked at me with an expression I'd never seen before, but it was clear that she did not grasp the full import of what I was saying. Nor, it was clear, did she want to.

"You are an insane, pompous fool," she said.

"That is unforgivable," I replied, and she fell silent.

When we returned, the sodden guests were eager to know to whom I'd spoken and what was said. I was not being coy when I said that it had been the President himself, but that we'd spoken in confidence. I smiled confidently at Muskie (surely he must have known), but he seemed barely to pay attention; rather, he watched Lionel, who at that point jumped up, spilling tiny potatoes and wine sauce down the front of his worn trousers. "Fuck you all!" I believe he said. "Fuck you all and fuck your fucking war!" At that, he left with not even a thank-you to Gretchen, who'd worked so hard to make my birthday a happy one, and with no apology to Luis, who rushed to scrub his thoughtless droppings from the carpet.

Until then, the mood in our warm little dining room had been one of mild curiosity and, I think, respect for my discretion, although the Swiss diplomat stared at me as if I were a spy in possession of valuable information. Now, however, the party was abruptly altered, overcome by a storm of unpleasantness. It was as if Lionel's anger had attached itself to all of us, even Ed and Jane, who then left hurriedly. Ed at least clasped my hand and wished me a happy birthday, but his departure had the effect of ending our evening in a hurry.

Beano demanded to know what Johnson had told me, and I whispered it to him so that the Swiss person could not hear. The diplomat glared at me, and then handed his card to Aileen, whose soft upper form was now perfectly traced by her wet blouse. Madeleine by now was hugging Gretchen, clutching her a little desperately, I thought, as she tried to swab my wife's onrushing tears. "This is the most awful, awful night," Gretchen kept murmuring, "awful, awful, awful," as if forgetting that it was my birthday party that had gone sour. As our guests fled, I remember having the oddest sensation: a mournful premonition that something had been lost for good in the social and intellectual intercourse of Washington—that this evening would somehow infect thousands of others in the years ahead. I understood that just as certainly as I understood that between Gretchen and myself, things had changed, too, perhaps for good.

*　*　*

As I relax by clicking through the forty or so channels on my little Sony, I find myself staring at a poster for the popular public television program *Washington Insights*. In the spring of 1970, when it began and I was asked to be a panelist, the half-hour was a novelty: a chance to watch informed journalists discuss the world just like ordinary people. At the time, I was not eager to participate; after all, I was not experienced in the medium and was fearful of making a fool of myself. We (those in the poster) never realized that we would become famous.

At the center is Chuck Moldine, who once wrote so passionately about urban matters for the *Philadelphia Bulletin*; his black face looks shiny but wise. To Chuck's right is Paul Vrovl, then a congressional reporter for *Time* magazine, already wrinkled beyond his forty-odd years. In front, seated, is Aileen Frugtsaft, who, thanks to a word dropped by me into Beano's ear, had just begun to cover the White House; her legs are crossed so that one wide thigh is half-revealed (Paul's hands rest playfully upon her shoulders). And there am I, wearing my trademark bow tie and a three-piece suit, my hair still blond and thick. To the side, arms folded, is Morton Manatie, our moderator and the program's creator, then nearly sixty. We are all smiling.

Even today, I can't explain our popularity, beginning with Paul Vrovl, who chain-smoked Pall Malls so that ashes smudged his cheap ties as he ranted in his whiny voice. Or for that matter Chuck Moldine. I always sensed great anger in Chuck, and although we never spoke about his rage, I think he appreciated that I often took his side. Chuck also understood that I disapproved of Paul's infatuation with Aileen, who was more than twenty years his junior and a favorite with viewers.

From the start, I felt comfortable on television; words flew from my lips as if they'd been scripted, and I appeared natural and animated to almost everyone. One critic wrote that I was "sharply articulate," and another that I had a "coldly studious concentration." An exception was Gretchen, although she said, "You were quite good" when I returned to O Street after our first broadcast. As the months passed, however, I would come home flushed with excitement and sexual energy, only to find that Gretchen had forgotten even to watch. I never told her how this disappointed me, but I'm sure that she knew. We continued to grow apart, and it did not help that, over the years, she brought little more than emotion to issues that occupied my waking thoughts. I could not forget that when I praised one or two of Nixon's sound appointments, Gretchen did not speak to me for a week.

It was the best of times to be a columnist, and yet sometimes I was nearly overwhelmed by what I felt was a wrenching upheaval in our nation's history. When hundreds of thousands of demonstrators, including Gretchen, went to the Mall to protest the war, many people said that I was unusually eloquent and restrained. Gretchen, to my regret, did not seem to care what I thought, nor did she notice when I called for a "cathartic consensus" and introduced that phrase to the language.

Part of Gretchen's indifference, no doubt, came from her laudable concentration on our family; Branny was three and a half in the spring of 1970, when I began my television work, and Gretchen herself had become pregnant again, to the surprise of both of us. But I also sensed Gretchen's indifference evolving into outright hostility. For instance, after I'd framed the *Washington Insights* poster that now hangs in my study, Gretchen resisted my plan to place it unobtrusively in the hallway. I thought it was an amusing decoration, and furthermore the group portrait—we all looked happily perplexed—was well done.

"Don't you think you're becoming just a little too full of yourself?" she asked. "Do you think I don't see you preening in front of your mirror?" And she added, "*There!* I've finally said it."

I cannot remember verbatim my reply, but the gist was this: "If you mean, am I proud of what I have accomplished in a few short years, yes. But if you mean, have I become vain, I would have to answer in the negative. The truth, Gretchen, is that you seem to take no pleasure in the strides I've taken, and you don't seem to realize that my success is something that you can share with me."

Rather than attempting a reply, which might have helped us to understand one another better, she ran from the room with a hooting sound. I wanted to follow, and re-examine our relationship. But I held back and tried to think what might be done to replenish the love we'd once felt for each other. I thought about Gretchen at Lorton Hills, riding through the wind as I urged my own mount to keep up; of our wedding day, when good friends like Madeleine and Jasper and Bob Hudnut surrounded two young people starting out together. I thought of Branny, now in his Montessori school, and how much joy the tyke gave us despite his problems (Branny seemed unable to form close attachments to others, and his teachers thought that he might have to be withdrawn from the school) and of the new life growing inside Gretchen.

I stood there alone, the poster in one hand and a ball peen hammer in the other. Perhaps I should have chased after Gretchen when the door slammed, and she dashed across O Street, but I knew that she would return and hoped that she would be calmer. A few minutes after I'd neatly driven a nail into the wall and affixed to it the framed poster that had caused our little row, Branny wandered downstairs and looked at my handiwork.

"Is that you, Daddy?" he asked, eyes wide.

I lifted Branny and hugged him, wishing that I had even more time to spend with him.

"That's me," I said, holding him so that he might see the five faces (which today have the patina of thirty-odd years) from a proper height. "How do I look?"

Branny smiled in a way that brought to my eyes a coating of tears. "He looks like Daddy," he said.

"So do you," I said, and hugged him with a father's desperate love.

* * *

While I'd been aware of Gretchen's dissatisfaction, I had no idea how deep it went and whether I might have done more to palliate it. After the birth of our daughter, Daphne (named after somebody in Gretchen's family), in early 1971, I'd hoped that matters would improve, but we seemed to draw farther apart over the next year, and it did not help that Gretchen taunted me with paraphernalia from the McGovern campaign while knowing of my friendship with Ed Muskie, his opponent in the primaries. I believe that both of us were puzzled by the cessation of our physical relationship.

Yet nothing could have prepared me for my homecoming in the early summer of 1972. I'd been in particularly good spirits. My day had included a searching conversation with Dr. Kissinger; in early evening, when my column on the China initiative was done (I gave it qualified praise), I had bumped into Aileen Frugtsaft, and one of us suggested a rapid nightcap at Pica's Roost.

We sat at a favorite table, damp with beery suds, and talked with the frankness of good friends about private matters. For the first time, I told Aileen that Gretchen and I were no longer living as man and wife; she could not mistake my meaning. Aileen then told me that Paul Vrovl, whose interest in her never slackened, had proposed marriage. She admitted that Paul, while not really able to satisfy her womanly needs (though he'd evidently tried), could provide other comforts, such as a house on Newark Street, with a wraparound porch. I could not mistake her meaning, either: Aileen was roughly my age, and for all the sensuality that she exuded, an important part of her life was unfulfilled.

No doubt I should have called Gretchen to say that I was running late; I was probably inconsiderate. What I most remember, when I returned to O Street, was that the front door was unlocked and that the house was unusually dark and still. At first, I feared that we'd been burglarized (my *Washington Insights* poster lay on the floor, the glass cracked). I tiptoed to our bedroom, and what I discovered was this: no Gretchen, no children. She, along with Branny and Daphne, had simply left. A note, in her childish scrawl, said, "I'm sick to death of waiting around for you—and also of being with you." I groaned aloud, as if to tell someone how she'd hurt me.

I was devastated by Gretchen's impulsiveness, and, at first, I had no idea where she was. In the morning, I called her parents, giving my voice a falsetto disguise, and was told (I believe that the Furlongs guessed it was me) that she was in Washington at a "private number." I worried that Branny and Daphne missed me, and it took the utmost concentration to hold fast to my standards of excellence in the column and on camera.

It was not until the next day that I learned from Madeleine Whitbridge where Gretchen had gone, and I sensed in Madeleine an enthusiasm for spreading the news. I hesitate to call Madeleine a gossip, for that connotes so many things that do not apply to her. But the truth, as I see it after so many years, is that Madeleine was unable to shut her fat mouth when she possessed sensitive information.

"Ah, Brandon, I believe that I can tell you about a certain person who is close to both of us," she said at once, affecting a mysterious tone.

I was at my desk. On a spike, numerous pink scraps attested to my unanswered telephone messages, each one neatly recorded by the girl who had come to work for me after I reluctantly decided to let Marge Cavanaugh go. Most were from prominent people, eager to tell me something of value.

"I am probably violating a promise by telling you this," Madeleine went on, "but it troubles me to see a couple in distress." She paused. "I believe I have given you hints of her troubled heart?"

I had a sharp memory of our little lunch a long time ago at Sans Souci, but, despite her warnings, I had never expected Gretchen to act so precipitately. I repeated to Madeleine my belief that the affection that Gretchen and I once had felt had not been wholly extinguished. I did not of course reveal that, as husband and wife, our relationship had not been conventional for some time.

"She has moved into Mrs. McSwigger's, but you mustn't tell her who told you this," Madeleine said at last.

Louisa McSwigger ran a boardinghouse in Cleveland Park, where the trees and grass did especially well, and Louisa McSwigger's Home and Shelter for Women (its formal name) was a refuge for women of good background. Sometimes, these were young women newly arrived in Washington, but in a very few cases they had fled from difficult husbands. There was also room for people like Gretchen, who presumably suffered from a form of depression and needed time to think.

My heart thumped and I fingered my pink telephone messages. "Our city is a very little one, in some respects," I said. "Perhaps there are others who know that she is staying at Mrs. McSwigger's?"

Madeleine coughed, and said, "You cannot rule out that sort of thing."

Then, when I mused aloud at the prospect of paying a surprise visit on the runaway Sladders, she coughed again, and said, "I do not think you would be wise to show up there, at least not right away."

One of my gifts is an ability to quickly size up a situation. This time, I felt a chill. "I think you are suggesting that we are experiencing more than a mere domestic squabble," I said finally.

"Brandon, I think you can guess," she said. "Gretchen is too well brought up to plunge headlong into a new relationship, but if I am to be honest with you, I must tell you that is her inclination."

I breathed deeply before uttering the words, "Lionel Heftihed."

Madeleine cleared her throat without coughing.

"That cannot be a total surprise," she said. "He has been of great comfort to Gretchen. And she admires his accomplishments and shares his deepest beliefs about the war. Furthermore, you can't deny that she is still very attractive. Even women notice her flawless skin, firm breasts, and perfect body."

I wished that she hadn't called, for there are some truths that a man does not want to face; or at least not while sitting at one's desk, staring at unanswered messages. My eyes filmed over as my fingers flicked past the names: Kissinger, Dobrynin, Ehrlichman, Hudnut.

"Madeleine, tell me the truth," I managed to say. "Do you think they have . . . you know?"

"Brandon, all I can say is that your wife has acquired that special glow that I, in a lifetime of experience, have come to recognize as its result. So it is a question that you must ask yourself."

It was of course a question to which I knew the answer. I had no idea what I would say to Branny or, when she was able to speak in an intelligible way, to Daphne. For some reason, I wept when I realized that I had never introduced Gretchen to my ailing parents, although they had gotten many photographs of our family.

"As usual, I'm in your debt," I said, coolly.

"You were splendid the other night," Madeleine replied,

referring to the television program, and I was grateful that she had paid attention to my prescient comments on the fighting in South Yemen.

Although I attempted to hide my circumstances for several weeks and tried to give Gretchen time to come to her senses, the condition of my marriage did not remain a secret. One day, Aileen Frugtsaft came to my office at the newspaper, sat upon my desk, and looked at me with a mournful visage.

"Say it ain't so," she said, her lips moving for a few seconds after she'd uttered the *so*.

"It is," I said, ruefully, "so."

Aileen had closed the door so that we would have the privacy that friends sometimes require. I was in the midst of writing another column on the value of the "China card," which Nixon kept playing with such skill, when she climbed back upon my desk, and sat in such a way that I was afforded a view of her I did not seek.

"Brandon, I'm so terribly sorry," she said, her eyes clouded with dejection.

I bowed my head, wondering if she was aware that she lacked undergarments, or if our stressful profession had made her forgetful. I told her that Gretchen's departure had come as a total shock, and she reached over and patted my head, then slid to the floor and embraced me in my chair. Her womanly warmth engulfed me.

"I feel closer to you at this moment than to anyone else in my life," she confessed, with another hug of friendship.

I felt much the same, although I wondered if Paul Vrovl, had he walked in, might misinterpret this moment between two friends, not that Paul had any claim on Aileen. I wanted always to do the decent thing, but I have learned that, all too often, our hopes may be defeated by our needs.

Fortunately, Gretchen's flight took place at a moment when I was exceedingly busy, not least because of the political conventions, which left me little time to torment myself. It was also during that summer of 1972 that my friendship with Bob Hudnut, now a senator, deepened; I was persuaded that he was an exception to Charles Whibley's declaration that "politics is the profession of the second-rate," and I saw him as a reflective man whose interests in arms control and women's rights were anything but superficial. In one column, I undoubtedly compared Hudnut to Jack Kennedy (I knew that women were drawn to the lean senator with the warm blue eyes), and if that seems too facile, it bears repeating that I'd known both men personally.

I no longer followed Bob's active bachelor life, but one night, when I'd stopped by his basement apartment on Capitol Hill, he surprised me by announcing that he'd gotten married. Not much later, he introduced me to Gwendolyn, a woman he had met in St. Louis during his Senate race. When I greeted her warmly, she put out a suspicious hand and refused to meet my steady gaze.

I found Gwendolyn to be surprisingly unlike the women Bob had been dating; she was tall, thin, very wealthy, and several years his senior. Gwendolyn seemed aware of my perplexity and made clear from our first meeting that she had no idea why Bob found time for me. When Bob and I were deep in a discussion of détente or Vietnam or politics or much more, and the hour was late, I could see weariness pinch Gwendolyn's narrow face and guessed that she couldn't wait for me to leave. When her face became tight, Bob's color would invariably darken.

After Gretchen moved out of our O Street house, I saw a lot of the Hudnuts, and I was grateful for Bob's kindness at a time when I was not particularly good company. (Bob was grateful when, in the weeks before McGovern was nominated, I included him in a list of worthy vice-presidential possibilities.) It meant much to me that Bob worried about my marriage, but I was startled one night when his thick fingers gripped my shoulders and he whispered, so that Gwendolyn could not hear, "There is a lot of very excellent pussy in this town."

* * *

For weeks, I'd hoped that the next knock on my door would be Gretchen's, but the procession of meter-readers, salesmen, roofers, tree-cutters, likely thieves, and would-be handymen, along with her continued absence, persuaded me that she was determined to make a statement; and during the winter of 1973, after the loneliest of holiday seasons, as the scandal that became Watergate began to grow, Gretchen demanded that I surrender our house, and move to a dwelling of my own. This request did not come directly from Gretchen, whose silence was by now getting on my nerves, but from her lawyer, whose cold letter added that Gretchen wanted to dissolve our marriage. This should not have come as a surprise, I suppose, and I knew that I'd not been the most attentive husband, but it still felt wrong. I had tried to include Gretchen in my life as much as possible, while taking note of her limitations, and I wasn't ready to give up. I also mulled, briefly, the fate of our possessions: Gretchen apparently was most eager to take an object that had special meaning for me: the signed photograph from Jack Kennedy. I immediately moved this cherished artifact to the safety of my office, where visitors were drawn to the luminous portrait (I resented that Gretchen stood between us) and the glitter of the PT-109 tie clasp.

At first, when I learned that she had moved into Mrs. McSwigger's, I heeded Madeleine's advice and kept my distance. If she'd begun a relationship with Lionel, I did not want to know the details. Lionel had, in my view, become increasingly disreputable, and while I applauded his modestly successful biography of Henry Adams, he then made the mistake of attempting a larger subject: the real "cost" of Vietnam. I could see how such pretension might affect impressionable young women, but Lionel was overreaching.

In any case, after hearing from Gretchen's lawyer, I realized that it was time to set aside any doubts concerning a visit to Mrs. McSwigger's, and so I set out on a warm Saturday morning in February to attempt a reunion. I'd hoped that Gretchen had watched *Washington Insights* the night before, because it had been especially lively.

Mrs. McSwigger's was deceptive, in that it appeared to be one of many such frame houses from the twenties with large lawns and ravenous squirrels. In fact, the house on Macomb Street, surrounded by beech and chestnut and maple trees, stretched out of plain sight in order to accommodate more than twenty bedrooms and nearly as many baths. Visitors entered by a double front door and then encountered a receptionist, who was installed behind a small desk, with a green felt top, a ledger book, and inkwells. One did not feel comfortable, as a member of the male sex, for many lodgers, as I have indicated, were there to get away from husbands and other problems.

The receptionist, a woman just emerging from the tunnel of her adolescence, was impressed when I revealed my identity; her sleepy eyes widened slightly, an effect augmented by the near absence of eyebrows. By this time, I'd found, many people twitched with vague recognition when they saw my face.

"I would like to meet briefly with my wife, Gretchen Furlong Sladder," I said, and smiled winningly.

My smile was not returned, but the receptionist opened the ledger, in which names were written in thick pen strokes—some crossed out, others added in ink of another shade: blue, black, and, more recently, a darkish green. I watched her finger pass along the page and noticed that their tips were ragged and that fragments of skin told the story of a nail-biter. I don't recall more about her, apart from her eyes, which, as I say, appeared to be somewhat naked in their browless fixity.

"Mr. Sladder," she said, "I see the words 'No spousal visits' next to her name."

"A misunderstanding," I replied, calm but resolute. "In the first place, it is inconceivable that she would not wish at the very least a glimpse of me, and in the second place, I have two small children here, from whom I have been separated against my will, although I have tried to be sensitive. I cannot imagine what those words in your little book actually mean, but I am quite sure that they cannot mean that, and I am quite sure that the police will agree that they cannot mean that."

The woman to whom I spoke looked at me with apprehension and I watched the fuzz of her lost eyebrows.

"Mr. Sladder, I am sure they mean just what they say," she said, oblivious to my implied threat.

"Miss—" I did not know her name, nor did I wish to acquire that peripheral information. "My request is only that you tell Mrs. Sladder I am here. Tell her that I do not insist on seeing her, but that I wish simply to set matters at rest between us."

We had reached an impasse, and although I was prepared to raise my voice, that turned out to be unnecessary. Even as the woman's eyes became hard and my face became flushed, I looked up at the wide staircase behind her and saw a familiar pair of legs, with a shapely muscularity that could belong only to Gretchen. Accompanying her were two beautiful children: Branny, scampering, and Daphne, in Gretchen's arms.

"How wonderful!" I said, in a voice that seemed to frighten the threesome. I saw Gretchen grip a banister.

I was in my Saturday garb in order to seem a more accessible and familiar figure: a tan windbreaker, a faded blue Lacoste shirt, rumpled khakis, and dirty bucks from Brooks Brothers. But I quickly sensed that our time apart had done nothing to expand the affection that I hoped lay beneath the surface.

Gretchen was obviously unready for the sight of me, but

after a few moments of uncertainty, Branny sped toward me and let my outstretched arms take him in. His cry of "Daddy!" spoke volumes, and I looked reprovingly at his mother. Daphne, who was only two, did not seem certain of my identity, but when Gretchen put her down, she offered a shy smile of the sort that brings the phrase "etched in memory" to life.

"Gretchen," I said. "I think you owe it to me to talk."

I felt Branny pushing as if to escape my grip, and Gretchen then suggested that we sit outside. In the moment it took me to agree, I had another surprise: Descending the staircase was a woman that I'd seen very recently, but in these unfamiliar trappings her name, for an instant, eluded me. Then it came: Gwendolyn Hudnut! I stared perhaps too obviously, taking in her short blond hair and her thin, tall, slightly ungainly walk. She seemed to have aged in a hurry. Bob and Gwendolyn had been a charmed, youngish couple just months before; now, she looked like an older, bitter woman of forty. Something, I could see, had taken its toll (a puffy, untrusting aspect), and I wondered what had brought her to Mrs. McSwigger's. When I said hello to Gwendolyn in my warmest voice, she did not appear to recognize me. I saw no reason to carry our dialogue any further.

Outside, the children played on the wintry brown lawn, enjoying the surprising warmth of this February day, while Gretchen and I sat side-by-side in two worn Adirondack chairs under a leafless maple. I noticed that she picked at the green, chipped paint.

"Since Daddy virtually paid for the house, it seems only fair that I should have it," Gretchen said at once.

I shook my head, not quite believing what had befallen us. Gretchen had not changed much in the nearly eight years that we'd been married, except that she had become more self-centered. Her blond curls had darkened and straightened, and I could see that the cleverness I had once imagined in her golden-brown eyes was actually a sort of cunning. Yet, the truth was that I still desired her.

"Are you truly determined to do this, Gretchen?" I asked, and reached for her small hand, which no longer included a ring.

She looked at me as if I were the stupid one, and sat on her hands.

"Brandon, why do you think I have been living for all these months at Mrs. McSwigger's? Why do you think I want a divorce?"

"To punish me?" I asked.

Gretchen lowered her voice and leaned toward me. The nearness of her lips, the very smell of her, affected me; I feared that my arousal might be visible through my rumpled khakis.

"Brandon," she said in a whisper, "why do you think I want to marry Lionel? Am I doing *that* to punish you?"

I must have quivered with shock; this was the first time that she'd spoken of marriage, or of Lionel. My stomach ached and my eyes became damp. Through a blur, I saw Daphne bouncing on Branny, and as I delighted in their infantile giggles and noticed, as if for the first time, how little they resembled one another, I wondered if Gretchen had ever—just once!—encouraged my own children to watch me on television.

"I wish you had understood me better," I said to her, swallowing many times. "I know that my job takes me away far too often from those who matter most to me." I raised my eyes to the two youngsters cavorting on the lawn, and waved. "I wish you understood how deeply I've felt the sacrifices I've made for my career."

Gretchen seemed to nod with sympathy, and I reached for her arm, which she refused to surrender to my care. If I knew that she was serious about ending our marriage, I also believed that a part of her still loved me.

"Of course you may see the children as often as you like," Gretchen said after a while.

I told her that I was eager to do so, and that I would find the time. In fact, I had been thinking of taking Branny and Daphne to Buffalo, a visit that had been promised and postponed numerous times; my own schedule had become increasingly complicated, and so had my mother's precarious health. My eyes moistened again as I said this, and I am quite certain that Gretchen's did, too. We sat there for some time, silently, sadly, mistily. It was, by any sensitive measure, an inappropriate moment to mention the Kennedy memorabilia, but Gretchen, without preliminaries, coldly demanded its return, saying of the Kennedys, "They were my *parents'* friends, at my *parents'* house." I gently shook my head, signifying no.

I looked at my watch, for I had promised Aileen Frugtsaft that I would let her know the outcome of this visit. Gretchen did not seem eager to prolong our meeting, and we both realized, I suppose, that there was not much to be said now that she'd stated her wants—or what she believed to be her wants.

My clear memory is of walking toward Branny and Daphne, then six and two, and wishing only to scoop them into my arms and protect them from adversity. I wanted them to know that their father loved them very much, and also wanted them to be proud. What I wanted most to tell them was that I had been having secret talks with NBC about becoming a permanent part of their news constellation. But my children ran to hide behind two rusted metal chairs across the lawn when I approached them. Even when I said good-bye, they went on playing their childish game, a form of hiding without seeking. In the distance, behind a chain-link fence, I saw Gwendolyn Hudnut, her face red from the sun, her life, too, closed off from my inquiring gaze.

*   *   *

For several months, my negotiations with NBC bogged down, but the network began to pursue me again as the Watergate affair, by the winter of 1974, swelled in importance. Morton Manatie begged me to continue with *Washington Insights*, and I was flattered, of course, and grateful to Morton, but I'd become increasingly unhappy with his program, in part because of its formulaic format and in part because of tension on the set. I had also been depressed for some time over my failure yet again to win a Pulitzer Prize.

People who watched us undoubtedly wanted to learn what insiders were thinking about Watergate, but I suspect that many of them simply enjoyed the bickering and guessed the truth: that some disputes, although they appeared to be over politics, were grounded in something per-

sonal, especially when they involved Paul Vrovl, Aileen
Frugtsaft, and myself.

At long last, Aileen had called a halt to her relationship
with Paul, which on several faltering occasions included
sexual intimacy. Paul then declared that she'd broken his
heart; he telephoned her incessantly and his arguments on
the air, never wholly rational at best, became increasingly
strained. My own friendship with Aileen, as well as her dis-
inclination to involve herself further with Paul, only increased his enmity.

It was in any case a difficult time for Paul. His editors at
Time had assigned someone else to follow Congress, leaving
his career to flounder. Aileen, meanwhile, was excelling at
the White House, and Paul, rather than taking pleasure in
her success, seemed only to resent it. The camera, too, was
cruel to Paul, who, as I may have indicated, looked every
one of his nearly fifty years and whose mouth curled downward in perpetual aversion; I watched with concern as a
spot beneath his right eye darkened and widened. He was
becoming hesitant when he spoke about Capitol Hill, and
Chuck Moldine took advantage of his stumbles to score lib-
eral jabs and the occasional uppercut. While it may appear
that Paul was right to suspect my intentions, as well as
Aileen's, he tormented her for months when he had, so far
as I know, no justification for doing so.

One particularly unpleasant night began in ordinary fashion, in the spring of 1974, three or four months before

Nixon resigned. Aileen had been a finalist for a Pulitzer Prize (as I was once more, for Commentary, defeated by an Asian woman from Los Angeles) and Moldine was on his high horse about what he kept calling the latest abuse of the Constitution by the White House. Aileen was plainly excited by the scandal. She wore her trademark short skirt, and had a way of turning to one of the two cameras, arching her back so that her silky blouse tightened whenever she castigated Nixon.

As usual, we'd been given Morton's questions in advance, and when he asked if we thought that Nixon should simply resign, our answers were at the ready: Chuck said yes; he could not recover. I argued that the Constitution should be followed as it was many years later with Clinton—impeachment by the House if it were warranted, then trial by the Senate. (I believe to this day that I was right.) Aileen arched her shoulders and revealed that Nixon was already considering resignation. At that, Paul turned and said, "You're all hysterical." The camera focused on Paul's contorted face as he added, in his nasal voice, "One of you just tell me exactly what Richard Nixon has done to merit this treatment!"

"How about bugging and burglary?" Aileen said.

"How about proving it?" Paul asked, his eyes fluttering. "And if you prove it, tell me that Johnson didn't do it. Tell me Kennedy didn't do it."

I broke in at this point to say that the Jack Kennedy I knew would never have stooped to such behavior, although I did not mean to imply that we had proof about Nixon; that was up to Congress to decide.

"We're talking about Richard Milhous Nixon," said Aileen, and she crossed her legs to reveal to some of us that she'd once more, absentmindedly, forgotten her undergarments.

Paul pounded the table and those of us in the small, hot, bright studio saw that his strained face was unusually red. A camera, callously, closed in.

"Admit it, Paul," said Chuck, in a mocking voice. "Nixon's a crook!"

"How *can* you deny it?" Aileen added, and as she shifted in her seat, I saw that a button of her blouse was missing and that she was not wearing a brassiere beneath its parting, silky folds. "It is obvious to everyone."

"Do you want to give a free pass to Presidents?" I said, and Aileen patted my hand in approval, her delicate fingers wrapping my thumb for an instant, massaging it.

Paul reached for a Pall Mall, although he'd never smoked on camera, and he lighted its tip with a shaky hand. I thought that it was important to emphasize that the Constitution itself was in jeopardy, but also that it remained a document that guides the nation; I had written something like that in my column a day or so before. As I said this, I noticed Aileen's separating blouse; only by averting my eyes could I avoid seeing what was indisputably the majority of a breast. Paul appeared to spy the same object, and became even more agitated.

"I just think that the American people want all this out in the open," Aileen said, as another button came undone. "I have very good sources inside the White House, and they tell me that the President is thinking more and more about taking a dramatic step."

When Aileen spoke of her superior sources, crisscrossing her legs in a way that embarrassed several of us, it was like a body blow to Paul. What shocked the audience of *Washington Insights* was not that Paul rose from his chair once more, or that he suddenly had two cigarettes dangling from his lips, and not even that he hissed that he could not bear this much longer. Who knew that Paul was not referring to the scandals? But when Paul said, "Where were you last night, Aileen? Out with your good sources?" the roots of his fury were fully exposed.

Aileen looked at me, for the truth was that she had been with me until quite late the previous night, innocently exchanging confidences at Pica's Roost. She had been attempting to comfort me, for I was still despondent over the deprivation of my wife and children, and was eager to replace them. But none of this could be explained at that moment, and none of it was.

Any doubts about my leaving public television ended two months later, when Paul collapsed. We'd been talking tiresomely of Nixon, whose defense of his tapes had reached the Supreme Court, and it was good luck that we had begun to record our programs; otherwise, the nation would have witnessed Paul clutching his chest and being carried away on a stretcher, gasping a defense of Richard Nixon.

As it turned out, we were able to leave Paul's comments

intact and continue, in abbreviated fashion, for the second half of the broadcast, although Aileen remained virtually silent. (Distraught, we all rushed to the hospital afterward.) I doubt that we would have completed our show if any of us had known that Paul actually had died moments after entering his ambulance, although, as Morton said, he would have wanted us to carry on as if he'd been fully present. For reasons that escape me, a cult of *Insights* watchers has since formed, and its adepts watch that episode and mouth the words of each of us in turn. The program, which I have never been able to watch, was dedicated to Paul's memory.

Despite the gossip, Aileen and I did not actually consummate our tie for some time, although I cannot deny that we had been, in a way all will understand, intimate. When the moment came, it felt entirely right and natural. I remember that Aileen locked the door to my office at the newspaper (the embittered Jervis Tramm had just walked by and did not even nod a greeting); and before I realized what was about to happen, she'd shed her clothing. I was startled at the sight of her completeness and found myself in full arousal. I recall wondering, as Aileen began her ministrations, if Russell Morgan Beadle had ever used this office for a similar purpose.

Of course I was fond of Aileen Frugtsaft; otherwise, I could not have countenanced my behavior. She was a good friend and helped me get through some rough patches, just as I may have helped Aileen get through some of her patches.

But as months passed and she hinted at marriage, I was frankly stunned, and told her so. "I know it's too soon," she said, clinging, I believe, to the hope that I would change my mind. I tried to dislodge that hope.

When we had that talk, we were sitting on a sofa in the living room of my house on Volta Place, the one which I inhabit today and where I write these lines. I'd recently bought the place, having surrendered O Street to Gretchen, and it had a strong smell of disinfectant, for cockroaches were everywhere and a dead rat had turned up in the cellar. Aileen's hand was unusually moist. Shortly before, we had been lovers (Aileen had been scratched by a faulty sofa tuft), and I suspect that we both felt a diminishment of our early passion; not only did our nakedness now seem a bit forced, but I thought more frequently about Paul. In my imaginings, Paul's senescing face was bright with anger as he espoused political views that I found simplistic. I found myself wondering what he would have said about the American evacuation of Vietnam, knowing that I would have to explore that grave situation myself.

"It is certainly, as you say, too soon," I told Aileen, not wanting to prolong this conversation and not really enjoying the prolonged sight of her freckled, unshackled breasts. "I am still not reconciled to the idea that my family has gone for good. I am still devastated by what happened to Paul. I'm deeply troubled by what's happening in Saigon as America pulls out, and I worry whether President Ford is up to the task." I paused, for I saw her staring at me as if I'd lost my mind. "And I'm still not prepared for all the changes in my professional life," a reference to my finally making the move from the self-righteous puddle of public television to the great lake of the NBC network.

That was certainly the truth, but I am afraid that it was more complicated than I'd let on. Not only did Aileen no longer arouse the physical side of me as she once had, but I had recently met someone else who did.

* * *

I met Alison Macciola in the spring of 1975. She was eighteen, a freshman at Yale , and she'd come to apply for a summer internship, which, as it happened, I'd just filled. But our conversation, which began as a job interview, was immensely stimulating and quickly skipped to other subjects, including the talents of Dr. Kissinger, the strategic petroleum reserve, and our imminent extrication from Vietnam. She noticed, behind my desk, the Kennedy photograph and tie clasp, and when I told her that I had only known him slightly, she instantly wanted to hear more. I remember being struck by the intelligence in Alison's dark eyes and her grasp of the world, as well as her naked ambition. She had pale, slightly plump legs, and I knew that we would see one another again. I was pleased when, within a day or so, she was hired by our newsroom as a copygirl.

In the beginning, Alison was an acolyte, curious about my personal tics as well as my thoughts, and her interest in the seemingly trivial details of my workaday life made me realize that my habits and methods, which have barely changed over the years, could be of interest to a budding journalist as well as the general reader. So I'll take a short break in this memoir to set them down:

Unless I have a breakfast meeting, my day begins with orange juice, dry toast, and coffee, in my kitchen. Quickly I scan the newspapers, looking for useful information. After taking copious notes, I head for the office.

Once there, I set to work, trying to keep up with incoming messages. (Those calls that are of obvious unimportance are handled by a young woman much like Alison.) Sometimes I stop in the newsroom to talk to a reporter who is in the thick of things; or I chat with old friends, although they rarely have time for pleasantries.

By then, it is lunch. I often meet with sources at Barkley's, that dark and welcoming oasis on lower Connecticut Avenue, named, with some irony, for Truman's vice president. (The first time I took Alison Macciola there, I watched her young eyes widen at every recognition; she seemed breathless at a first encounter with Senator Hudnut.)

After lunch, I return to my office; stacks of books and publications are scattered hither and thither, with markers inserted in key places—possibly an interesting thought that has caught my eye. More than once, I have cited Macaulay's view that "to be a really great historian is perhaps the rarest of intellectual distinctions." Quickly, I scan new messages to determine which ones need immediate attention. Usually, there is a call from my syndicate, or from my television producer. By the time I return the most urgent calls, it is already three o'clock, and time to get on with the column.

I still eschew the word processor, and work on a worn IBM Selectric, having surrendered my portable Hermes to the junk heap. (I am not a good typist, but I have advanced beyond the hunt-and-peck method.) The process of finding a topic was—and is—mysterious, and on those rare occasions when I am stumped, I often use a favorite device, such as an imaginary dialogue with a deceased statesman (often Dean Acheson); a cultural moment, such as a movie (*Star Wars*, *Forrest Gump*); and, possibly too often, I have fallen back on Santayana's warning. (I was not amused when Aileen Frugtsaft, during a taping, turned to me and said that those who forget Santayana's warning are doomed to hear it repeated.)

When I write, I begin slowly, but pick up speed after completing the first few sentences; my middle passages are sometimes a struggle, especially when I sense that I am about to pen an insightful thought. Somehow, I know when I have reached the requisite eight hundred words that my syndicate expects, whereupon I rip the sheets from the typewriter and hand them to my girl for proofreading and comment. If all is in order (and often we change a word, or the placement of a comma, to bring more clarity to my opinions), she delivers it to the eighth floor, where it is dispatched—once by teletype, now by today's computerized miracle—to my subscribers. Soon after, my work belongs to the public and is beyond recall.

"It is fascinating," Alison sometimes said to me of my life, and I would nod my head in pleased agreement. I looked forward more and more to her visits and her strangely wide smile, and at first I thought that she was unconscious of the pleasure she gave when she kissed my cheek and leaned toward me, or stroked my neck playfully when we discussed something I'd written and told me how much she'd learned from it. It seemed an accident when her fingers brushed me.

Certainly, I was aware of the difference in our ages and status; I could not wholly ignore that Alison had a distinctly different set of historical references. Yet, other factors came into play. From the start—and it did start almost at once—the physicality of our tie was intense; she inflamed me as if I were a teenager. Once, quoting the *Iliad*, I jokingly whispered into Alison's tiny ear Chapman's lines on Achilles, who "drew his lance, his father's spear,/Huge, weighty, firm, that not a Greek but he himself alone/Knew how to shake . . ." The summer was soon over, and I did not realize how much she'd come to mean to me until she returned to college for her sophomore year.

I tried to be discreet, knowing that others might be hurt. But discovery was probably inevitable, and one night in late August, on upper Wisconsin Avenue, we were leaving an amusing movie (something with Jack Nicholson, who played a mental patient) when we ran into Aileen Frugtsaft, who looked weary and sad. Aileen did not seem to hear the compliments we tossed at her for a story she'd written about Gerald Ford's inner circle. Rather, she looked at me menacingly, then leaned forward and whispered, "You've got a fat head, Brandon, and your stomach is getting there, but I never thought you'd be putting your fat prick into a child." Words like that are the sort that ruin friendships, and they undoubtedly damaged ours.

Alison, of course, was extraordinarily mature despite her years, and over the next few semesters, I would see her on weekends, during school breaks, whenever possible. I know that during the 1976 presidential campaign, as Jimmy Carter and Ford debated about Eastern Europe and the receding scandal, I felt happier than I had in years. "You're my little puppy," Alison sometimes said, with a giggle and enormous smile, "always panting." I know that our alliance offended old friends like Madeleine Whitbridge, and I understood why it distressed Aileen Frugtsaft, who was all too aware of her childbearing parameters. But I was willing to pay that price in the belief that I'd found a soul mate. Alison, for instance, may have been the first to see that my columns were a continuum; she encouraged me to gather them for the book that became *Incline and Precipice*, which, no doubt helped by my regular appearances on NBC, was a *New York Times* best-seller for three weeks in the summer of 1977.

When I eventually asked Alison to be my wife, she accepted with apparent enthusiasm, although it troubled us both that her father and mother, who did not have formal educations, refused to have anything to do with it. (It struck me as curious that both the Furlongs and Macciolas took that stance vis-à-vis me.) Alison's parents lived in Baltimore, and we met several times, but while our get-togethers were courteous enough, we had nothing to talk about and I was almost always in a rush to leave. I believe that they hated that I was not of Italian heritage, not a Catholic, and divorced. Alison thought that they simply couldn't stand me. We had in any case decided to put off a wedding until Alison graduated, which was for the best because of my own tragedy: my mother's death, which was unexpected. Although Mother had been ailing for several years, her passing affected me almost as a physical shock.

I had not been exceptionally close to my parents, but I ought to have had some hint that matters were near a final phase. I knew nothing; *nada*. Because my father had never bothered to learn my unlisted number, I did not even get the news until the following morning, after I'd finished my juice, coffee, and toast, and had scanned my messages and newspapers. My girl then handed me a pink message slip, reading, "Your father called to say that your mother died yesterday evening, and you might want to attend her funeral."

I shut the door at once, and for several minutes, I stared silently at the walls, my shoulders heaving; then I did not hesitate, but told my girl to book airline reservations and a room in a good hotel. I entertained the thought that Alison should accompany me, but quickly put it out of mind. Although I believed then that Alison and I were, in a very real sense, collaborators in mind and spirit, I did not want to put her through such a wrenching occasion. After all, she had never met my mother and was also in the midst of a set of difficult midterms.

As for my parents, I wish that I'd done more to close the distance between us. They were not sophisticated, but they worked hard and tried to live good lives. (After some years at the grocery store, I learned, Dad had gone to work for the Postal Service, and only recently retired.) My father, however, still treated me as a stranger, even at the funeral, where his keening grief was noticeable to the few friends and neighbors who attended (some of whom stared at me with curiosity, having seen me on television). Afterward, he seemed to want to get away from me when I comforted him, or attempted to show him pictures of Branny and Daphne, capturing their lives from infancy onward. I was shocked at how my father had aged (he was nearly seventy, and had lost lots of weight), and wondered if his defeated face, and the thin white hair above it, was a preview of my own eventual visage. "I'm so sorry, Father," I said, before I left for the airport, "so very sorry," and I tried without success to weep onto his shoulder. We did not, to my sorrow, speak again for many years.

*   *   *

My birthday, in the fall of 1979, tossed me into my fifth decade, and I'm not sure that I landed well. Whenever I objected to spending time with one of Alison's college chums (my stomach knotted), she liked to remind me that she was twenty-three to my forty, and the distance between our years seemed somehow to widen. My relations with the White House, which were already sour (Jimmy Carter's smallness annoyed me), became acrid soon after a few dozen American diplomats were taken hostage in Teheran. In several columns, including a dialogue with Dean Acheson, I scolded Carter for not taking decisive and, if need be, deadly steps to free the prisoners—and urged him to demonstrate a bit of backbone. Worst of all, the rush of events in the next few years (the Russian invasion of Afghanistan, the Arab oil embargo, Brezhnev's declining health, the election of

Ronald Reagan) demanded more of my attention, and left me less time to be with my children, Branny and Daphne.

Once or twice, I brought Branny to the NBC studio on Sunday mornings, thinking that he'd enjoy watching me tape our program, but when he began to trip over cables and play little pranks with cue cards, he had to be removed by a technician and was no longer welcome. Similarly, when he visited my office, he quickly became bored, sullenly wandering around the smoky fluorescence of the newsroom until he found "Uncle Beano," as Branny called him. He showed no interest at all in my profession.

Gretchen, meanwhile, had to my surprise gone to law school and, assisted by good looks and family connections, had actually become a limited success at one of Washington's better firms. I was proud of her. As for Lionel Heftihed, I am sorry to say that his work went steadily downhill after his little Henry Adams biography. His Vietnam book was thrashed by several critics, and although I probably should have recused myself, I felt it was my duty to take him to task for his poor historiography, speciousness, and shoddy prose. It sold poorly, and after that, or so I heard, he was attempting to write about the journalism of Washington. I felt no rivalry with Lionel, but I did sometimes suspect that he might have said something to turn my children against me. (He and Gretchen were childless—impotence? a low sperm count?)

By the early eighties, Branny had swapped his hyperactive boyhood for a disturbed adolescence. I knew that it was commonplace for fifteen-year-olds to experiment with drugs, but Branny seemed too eager to test James Russell Lowell's observation that "one thorn of experience is worth a whole wilderness of warning." I disliked his friends, especially a classmate with the odd name of Wing (she had dirty hair and violet lips), who undoubtedly awakened the carnal side of Branny's life. When I pointed a finger at his stepfather, Lionel, Gretchen would accuse me of alienating my son. But it was my distinct impression that the reverse was true—after all, Branny had been alienating me for fifteen years. Still, with her bag of brand-new law school tricks, I found it increasingly difficult to argue with Gretchen. When she used important-looking legal stationery to demand the return of my Kennedy keepsake, which became more precious with each passing year, I ignored her.

By contrast, Daphne was "Daddy's girl," and as a youngster, she collected photographs of me. (The one she had me autograph for her chums was an informal shot that showed me at my desk, with a paperweight baseball; my hair is tousled, my bow tie is askew, and my smile is a little hard to read.) Everyone was fond of the artlessly affectionate Daphne, who, unlike her older brother, enjoyed Sunday mornings at the television studio. After one of our programs, when she was about ten, she leaped into the lap of Senator Hudnut, who'd been a guest, and he pronounced her "adorable" and hugged her as he would have hugged his own child.

The one person who did not respond to my children was Alison, who had done well for herself almost from the moment that she'd graduated with distinction. With what I now realize was remarkable speed, Alison fashioned a career as a Washington literary agent. Congressmen, impressed by my popular collection of columns, called her when they wanted to anthologize their thoughts; so did journalists eager to memorialize a tedious foreign assignment. Almost without realizing it, we became a Washington couple (a "power couple," as the vulgar phrase had it). I believe that we were a striking pair, perhaps a little too dashing for our conservative town.

Branny and Daphne, however, thought that they detected something "sneaky" about my young wife, which I saw as residual loyalty to their biological mother and which Alison interpreted as deep antipathy. "I'm sorry," she said far too often, "but if your obnoxious kids were to get run over by a truck tomorrow, I think it might actually help our relationship—not that I'd ever wish for such a thing." Her insensitivity on this score—and her insane remark that Daphne bore a curious resemblance to Lionel—was the sort of thing that complicated our lives. Sometimes it was as if I lived in separate, parallel places: my work, my domestic life, and, as time passed, my friendship with Bob Hudnut.

I'd made no secret of my interest in a Hudnut presidential candidacy, but I was always aware that Bob's personal life was a liability. At century's end, we are supposedly blasé about the sex lives of our leaders, but I have never been able to set aside my intense interest in the subject. I frequently urged Bob to remarry, if only to address the rumors that his ex-wife had been spreading. After leaving Mrs. McSwigger's, Gwendolyn had returned to St. Louis, where she'd undergone years of intense psychiatric treatment; from her assisted living facility there, she'd written letters that made fantastical claims, notably that Bob had stolen her fortune for his last campaign. She told people that Bob was not like other men, and that he liked to wear the costumes of Las Vegas showgirls. (When Bob heard about this, his guffaws were loud and long.)

Bob was certainly magnetic; several women at the newspaper had attached his photograph to partitions by their desks, as if he were a movie star rather than a talented legislator. (Aileen Frugtsaft, her aspect now desperate, had two Hudnut photographs.) A favorite showed the senator in front of the Capitol, wearing tight blue jeans with a noticeable bulge and a jerkin, his signature hair tossed by the wind and a briefcase slung casually over a shoulder. To me, Bob was simply a man, flawed like the rest of us and unable fully to come to terms with his cravings—but not, as Gwendolyn said, "a sicko psycho."

It was sometime near the end of Reagan's first term, I believe, that I first noticed Bob's habit of appropriating a phrase, or sometimes considerably more, from one of my columns; and although I was flattered, it made me uneasy that he seemed to make no distinction between his thoughts and mine. One afternoon, I stopped by Bob's shadowy office in the Dirksen Building and, in the most offhand way, asked him about these borrowings.

"The other day," I said, "I described Mrs. Thatcher as a surefooted shortstop who seems to be fielding line drives. The next day, you called her a third baseman fielding hard grounders, but the basic idea—"

Bob's face took on a surprisingly moronic aspect, as if

he'd not followed my point, and then he tried to finish my sentence. "There are only a few basic ideas out there, Brandon," he declared. "You of all people should know that."

I tried to ignore his little gibe about my column, which some complained had become repetitive. "There may be only a few ideas, but there is a shifting context," I said, adding, for emphasis, "For instance, nothing has changed more than our bilateral relations with the Soviet Union."

Bob gave me a patronizing look and brushed his tawny hair with stubby fingers that always spoke to me of the lineage of peasants. "You know, Brandon, this may impress your readers, but I don't give a rat's ass about your context and your bilateral relations. I mean, what the fuck are you talking about?" Bob grinned, and his Missouri twang faded in and out like a weak radio signal.

My eyes wandered, from his burgundy desk to the coffee-stained rug to portraits of Missourians, and I breathed deeply and thought (a vague, not quite realized thought) that I smelled a familiar perfume.

"You've used a lot of my material," I said, not backing off. "My ideas, my language."

"And that makes you pissed?" he said, with ingratiating laughter.

I conceded that it was not, after all, exceedingly troublesome; I just wanted some credit. And after that admission, Bob was surprisingly bold: "Maybe you ought to just write my speeches for me," he said, his eyes mischievous. "I mean, if I'm going to try this thing"—now his gaze was earnest, for he meant an eventual run for the White House—"I ought to start sounding smarter than I am."

For the first time since I'd known him, I was nonplussed. While I could justify acting as informal Hudnut adviser (friend, patriot), I could not defend myself (impartial columnist) as a clandestine Hudnut employee. Yet Bob was, undeniably, a pal, and I thought of the times that we'd talked into the night about America. I thought of how he'd comforted me when Gretchen had walked out and the slanders he had endured from poor Gwendolyn. Furthermore, since he seemed to have little compunction about stealing from me, I did not see how my formal participation could alter the equation. If this seems like sophistry, so be it.

"If I write what I genuinely believe," I said, speaking mostly to myself, "I imagine there is nothing wrong with that. I could even praise your speeches," I added. When Bob's head took on a seesawing motion, I continued, "I mean, these are issues that we've discussed because we're friends and believe many of the same things, right?"

His sly smile changed to one of pleasure, and with surprising quickness we agreed that the speeches would range from arms control to urging tough love in poverty programs to a rededication to our neighbors in Latin America. I'll admit to suffering a spasm of vanity: From the ephemera of mere words, I thought, I could lay hands on history itself.

Yet, it is the truth, so help me, that even then I had my reservations about Bob; the twitch in his leg, for instance, and his occasional dazed look, which I attributed to his short attention span; and his private life: Bob told me that he saw himself as a helpmate to the poor—"an ambassador from the nation of learning," in another apt phrase borrowed from me—but I wondered about the young African-

American women who lounged about his basement apartment on Capitol Hill and seemed only to watch television and eat potato chips. One of them was a girl of about thirteen with milky skin and pigtails; she once handed me Bob's own card, and on the other side was her name—Lascala—and a telephone number, written in pencil. "If you ever want to give me a lesson, sir, I do love to learn," Lascala said, and I could not meet her cheeky stare when she handed me the shiny cardboard rectangle. As I slipped it into a pocket, I thought for the first time in years about Zoe Wicksworth and felt a kind of shame.

One late-summer night in 1984 (I had just returned from San Francisco, and the disastrous Democratic Convention that nominated Mondale and Ferraro), Bob and I sat in my small backyard on Volta Place, drinking cold beer from bottles that Alison had fetched. As cicadas rattled our tiny universe, I thought that he looked a little too longingly at Alison's departing form, her luminous calves (she wore a short, leafy-green skirt that climbed up her pudgy legs). In the moist darkness of the city, he suddenly referred to my first wife, Gretchen, as "prime pussy," and despite his apologetic grin, and my chuckle (and my thought: Take that, Lionel!), it was deeply distasteful. Several minutes later, Bob rose quickly from the lawn chair. "I must go," he said, adding enigmatically, "Life beckons."

After shaking his hand, I remember feeling a sort of melancholy. "You're like a jealous lover, whenever he leaves," Alison said, in a husky whisper. Not for the first time, her teasing got under my skin and I told her so. I tried to hug her, and was aroused in a wobbly way as my hands climbed under her skirt and gripped her soft buttocks. But she pulled away, as she often did, this time almost angrily, and whispered something that sounded like: "You're getting too old and fat for me, bub."

*   *   *

For far too long, I'd lost touch with Madeleine Whit-bridge, possibly because her loyalty to the Furlong family superseded her affection, such as it was, for me, and possibly because we'd begun to move in different circles; although we'd now and then spotted each other across roomfuls of people, I'd often find myself among men and women who'd never heard of her. But my affection for Madeleine was undiminished, and I was delighted when she called me on a fall morning to suggest lunch. "Alas, Sans Souci is gone," she said, and I suggested Barkley's, although she felt little kinship with the journalists and political consultants and sports figures who ate heavy food there. She arrived first (I spotted her large silver necklace), and when I got close to her table, as pewter platters sailed about, I saw that she'd aged considerably. Her hand, when I took it, felt cold, as did her cheek, when I bent to peck it.

"You've gotten older, Brandon," she said. I knew that my hair, once blond and wavy, had begun to gray and thin (on television, one could see terrifying pinks of scalp at certain angles) and that wrinkled skin now radiated from my eyes and mouth. I must have been forty-six or so, but the pressure of work took its toll. When Madeleine asked for a Chardonnay, I did the same.

We began lobbing pleasantries across the breadsticks, although I had to speak a little louder because Madeleine's hearing was failing; time is so mean-spirited. She told me that she'd not been well (I didn't press for details) and that Ariadne, her daughter, who was only a name and blank spot to me, had moved to Singapore with her husband, Claus, evidently a German businessman. I'm always made uneasy when people refer to people I don't know by their first names.

"Now and then I see Gretchen, who is looking ever more beautiful," Madeleine continued, and her eyes fastened on mine. "She and Lionel do not seem very happy, though; one hears rumors, which I won't repeat." I pleaded with her to repeat at least one rumor, but she was unyielding. "You will be glad to know," she said, "that Gretchen has just won a case that may be worth many millions and that Lionel is almost finished with his book about journalism in our town." She added, as if confiding, "I understand it is very good and wise."

I doubted that, and told Madeleine about myself: My column by then appeared in nearly four hundred newspapers worldwide, my contract with NBC had been renewed for another three years, and at least once a week I flew someplace to speak in return for a handsome fee. I said that Alison and I were happy, although childless, and that she was becoming ever more successful with her small literary agency, most recently by assembling a volume of speeches that encapsulated the philosophy of Bob Hudnut.

"As you know," Madeleine said, a little sharply, "I'm not really acquainted with Alison—with the entire Alison phase of your life." She paused, and smiled a little sadly. "Yet it is appropriate that you mention her, Brandon, for she is one of the reasons I have suggested that we have this over-due lunch."

I remember, for some reason, that she then patted her napkin to her mouth as if she'd eaten something, when in fact the Chardonnay was about to arrive, and that the clatter in the large room, dark even by day, seemed to evaporate. She moistened her diminished lips with her tongue and looked over her left shoulder, as if someone might be eavesdropping. This was certainly a habit she'd picked up from her husband, Willy Whitbridge, who was famed for his tradecraft, but it is also a habit that many who live in Washington—at least those of us who run our town—acquire. It is a very small community (when you exclude those tragically neglected neighborhoods east of Rock Creek Park) and we tend to spot one another everywhere. During our meal, I greeted several acquaintances, among them the former Swiss ambassador who had been a guest in my house when Gretchen and I were together, a Washington Redskin, two members of the Reagan cabinet, an elderly lawyer who had worked for Lyndon Johnson, and a man I thought, mistakenly, was Walter Mondale.

"Alison seems like an attractive girl," Madeleine went on, fondling the stem of her wineglass, her fingers nervously leaping to her white hair. "Clothing is not modest in this day and age, and it is very obvious that she has a spectacular figure."

She was correct (I thought of Alison's soft limbs, her upright bosom and scarlet nipples), and as if sensing my embarrassment, she glanced at the menu, taking her time before she ordered fettuccine with a light tomato topping. Although I wanted to lose weight, I asked for the same, with a tasty meat sauce.

"I am relieved to learn that Alison is Bob's literary agent," she said then, "for that would explain why they are so often seen together."

My stomach heaved very slightly. "Many people say that it will be a book of some importance," I replied after a few seconds. "There will be a lot of interest in his best speeches if he seeks a higher office in '88 or '92."

Madeleine nodded. "From what I have heard of his speeches," she said, "they are unusually thoughtful."

I nodded noncommittally.

Madeleine shook her head several times, and said, "People say that your wife often goes to Bob's office and stays for hours." Her tongue retrieved a droplet of wine. "One knows, of course, that Bob has a reputation. Did you know that he was very fond of Gretchen?"

I smiled reassuringly, even as the words "prime pussy" leaped into my mind. Nevertheless, I felt confident that

Gretchen had never strayed from me. As for Alison, I could no more imagine a liaison between her and Bob than one between myself and, well, Gwendolyn Hudnut. Alison had told me that Bob's attraction was a mystery to her, and, furthermore, that he was nearly twenty years her senior (a discomfiting reminder that the same was true of me). But Alison's whereabouts were frequently not known to me. Nor could I deny that our intimacies, after seven years of marriage, had diminished in intensity and frequency, although my needs remained urgent.

"No, it is nothing to worry about," I said, even as Madeleine's thin eyebrows arched slightly and I wondered who could be spreading those vicious lies.

I recall that several more luncheon patrons stopped by our table and greeted me warmly, including one or two whose names I couldn't recall, and that waiters filled our glasses attentively as a pleasant sense of belonging overtook me. On a napkin, I jotted down some interesting thoughts about Gorbachev, most of which would make their way into a column and over the airwaves. (I had missed a chance to meet in Moscow with Chernenko.) Soon, we were slipping strands of fettuccine into our mouths, silently, until Madeleine cried out because a microscopic speck of tomato sauce had landed on her white blouse. For a moment, she seemed defeated by that reddish dot, but then she turned to me again and gave me careful scrutiny.

"You continue to be very good on television," Madeleine said. "My friends and I agree: You are by far the most thoughtful, witty, and literate columnist in America."

I thanked her for those kind words, and repeated the

idea—was it Emerson? Holmes? Hobbes?—that, by a peculiar weakness of human nature, people generally think too much about the opinion that others form of them. But even as I took pleasure in Madeleine's praise, I felt an odd sort of uneasiness, one that had been creeping up on me more often. I had long dreamed of reaching this stage in life—my ideas discussed at Washington dinner tables and my name known—yet something, I felt, was lacking; and not knowing what only made its absence more painful. Many men of high achievement are tormented by a sense of incompleteness; that is the impression I've gotten in my searching, bilateral conversations with three Presidents and many foreign leaders. But that was small consolation; our doubts, Shakespeare wrote, are traitors.

It was so good to see Madeleine, even if, as it might appear, she was the bearer of unhappy suspicions. Neither of us could have known that it would be our last lunch together, but if we had, I doubt that our conversation would have been very different. I remember telling her about my plan to write more frequently about the subtle connection between sports and politics. I told her that Daphne, now fourteen and in junior high, was studying ballet and excelling at field hockey. From the way Madeleine lowered her eyes and saddened her voice, I realized that she'd heard about Branny, and of his arrest for the stupid prank of calling in bomb threats to airports. Madeleine then told me that Tobias Goldenstein, whom I hadn't seen in years, was giving himself a seventieth birthday party, to which I hadn't been asked. I had a sharp memory of Esther, Tobias's daughter, and wondered what had become of her. I must have spoken those words aloud, for Madeleine said, "I haven't followed her life, Brandon, but I am sure that she will be present at such a major celebration. People who have seen her in New York say that she is still very beautiful, and of course she is a skilled and influential editor."

It was, I realize now, the perfect farewell, for we'd caught up with so much. When coffee and little cakes were set down and I asked Madeleine about Jasper Munroe, her old friend, her eyelids trembled; I could not at first hear in the racket of food and gossip all around. Then I realized that she was saying, "We all get on, don't we? And we don't come back," and I saw that her eyes were closed.

*   *   *

I f one took seriously all that is said about oneself, it would not be possible to function in this town, and I shrugged off the prattle about Alison. Of course I noticed the distant, oppressed look in her eye; and certainly I hated it whenever she said, "You're so fucking full of yourself," and that we quarreled over our choice of friends, our furnishings, her short skirts. She was also, I believe, annoyed at my failure to achieve a pregnancy with her, although my fertility score-card was obviously superior to hers and things might have gone better if she'd taken the initiative just once.

I wasn't really suspicious, but after my lunch with Madeleine, I couldn't resist an occasional mention of Bob Hudnut's name, just to gauge Alison's reaction. I recall watching *Washington Insights* (now a shadow of its former self) and stroking her pudgy thighs as I shared my thoughts, which I've since revised, about Nicaragua and the contras, saying, "I wonder what Hudnut will say about that." When her limb tensed, I felt like a human polygraph. Then, softly, almost hissingly, she asked if I planned to keep writing Bob's speeches. I clutched her thigh in shock, for I had meant to keep this an absolute secret. "How," I asked, "did you know?"

She giggled contemptuously and said, "The literary world in Washington is such a tiny one."

"It could ruin me—utterly—if anyone were ever to find out," I said, emphasizing every word.

At that, she gripped me with her slender fingers. "Why didn't you tell me? Don't you trust me?" she asked, and her dark, intelligent eyes became quite angry as her fingers tightened, painfully. "Furthermore," she added—a little menacingly, I thought—"you've taught me better than anyone that only your friends can really have you by the balls." Then she squeezed.

Gnats of jealousy sometimes swarmed about, but I would brush them away. Now and then, I would intercept glances that were difficult to interpret, although inexplicable glances are part of life in Washington. One November night, Alison and I went to a cocktail party at the home of a high official (one, incidentally, who continues to play an important role in the defense community). It was raining and I'd not seen a pondlike puddle as we walked from our car to the wooden steps of our host's Cleveland Park house, stepping in it, perhaps because Alison and I were squabbling about something ("Do you ever stop your fucking name-dropping?" she'd said when I'd simply told her who'd be there). In any event, we soon headed to opposite sides of the room, mingling with guests and clutching glasses of wine, my left foot soaked. At one point, my host pulled me aside to tell me about an idea he'd worked out during his years in the private sector: producing pocket-sized nuclear weapons for the battlefield. As he sketched the device on a napkin—"One kiloton, just a firecracker," he said—I looked up and saw, of all people, Esther Goldenstein, my friend from the lost, beloved *New Terrain*. Her hair was longer and she was older (after all, it had been some twenty years), but she was beautiful, just as Madeleine had reported. We hugged with genuine warmth as she murmured, "How strange!" and clasped my hand, adding, "Oh, Brandon, you've done so well."

I said that luck had played its part, and that I regretted having lost touch. It seemed obvious to me, as she got closer, her eyes wide with Jewish mournfulness, that her life had not been easy; her welcoming smile became a grimace. My heart raced with affection.

"You never answered my letters," she said.

I'd meant to, of course, remembering how things get misplaced in the press of work, and how it then feels too late. As I thought this (or perhaps expressed it aloud), I started to ask Esther about herself, and to tell her that I missed her in the way one misses vanished friends. Was she married? Before I could speak, however, I felt a tug at my elbow, and was face-to-face with another old acquaintance: Jasper Munroe, who was about to retire from the Senate and was in search of fresh conversation. Jasper held on to me as he attempted to remember my name, and it was then that Esther moved closer and whispered, her lips touching my ear, "Is something going on between Senator Hudnut and your new wife? I heard that from our old friend," and as I separated myself from Jasper, she pointed to someone I'd not noticed: Lionel Heftihed, whose prematurely lined face was additionally creased by a smirk. Lionel, who had come to this heretofore excellent party alone, pretended not to see me.

"It's a damned lie," I said, and stared into her gloomy smile. But as I told Esther about my wife, and of my pride in her accomplishments, those gnats of jealousy began to swarm again, and my mood was not helped when Esther told me that she had read a few chapters of Lionel's work-in-progress about journalism—now entitled "The Amoral Compass"—and that it was brilliant. "Part of it is about you," she added mysteriously, but I was incurious. Across the room, I saw Alison, her pretty face tilted with interest as she listened to a C.I.A. man who was eager to entrust his *pensées* to paper. The C.I.A. man had an erratic gray goatee and reptilian eyes. Alison, who was then about twenty-nine, looked entranced; her dark hair shimmered.

"I would love to meet her," Esther said. I was not, however, eager to introduce them, and suddenly I wanted to escape her, just as I had years before, perhaps because her stare and her interest in Alison made me so uncomfortable. I'd suddenly realized that the sadness I had seen in Esther's eyes, that glimmering melancholy, was actually a judgment of me.

I am writing this many years later, enjoying the peace of my private study—"a kind of clean bare antechamber to heaven," in J. B. Priestley's words—and perhaps I am trying to postpone the act of further committing the past to paper. It is far more pleasant to study the mementos that give life some meaning, such as my many citations for commentary, which mean more to me than the Pulitzer Prize I've been repeatedly denied. I sometimes think that change arrives so slowly that it is possible to dodge it; then it overwhelms, such as when little Branny disgraced himself just before the Christmas holidays—arrested at the corner of Fourteenth and Euclid streets for something having to do with drugs. It seemed an impossible embarrassment for a Sladder offspring (he managed to get both our names into the newspapers), but at the same time, I was proud of Branny for wanting, as I understood it, to stand on his own two, unsteady feet, away from his father's shadow. When Branny was arrested, he called his mother, not me; and at his arraignment, to his credit, he wanted Gretchen and his deeply disturbed girlfriend, Wing, not me. Through it all, his stepfather, Lionel, who deserved much of the blame, was notably silent.

By contrast, Daphne continued to make me proud. She was surrounded by friends and excelled at sports, no doubt a heritable talent from her mother. But I worried that she was unaware of the sexual power she wielded—even at the age of fifteen—which was terrifyingly obvious to me. On our weekend outings at shopping malls, when I saw young men staring at Daphne with animalistic appreciation, I'd advise her to be more modest (she favored halter tops and tiny shorts), but she'd shrug off my pleas with girlish giggles as she darted into Nordstroms and Limiteds and Benettons and bought more of the same. I feared that one of the adolescent males Daphne saw for an evening of aimless, teenage amusement might rob her of her innocence.

As it turned out, my life changed quite predictably. I recall that the weather in the spring of 1986 was magical, with cherry blossoms in plump pinkness and a sunny warmth filling the city. I'd come to work early to finish up a column describing an interesting observation that Bob Hudnut had made about the Middle East (comparing Israel to the Amazin' Mets of 1969). I was weary, because I then had to sketch out yet another Hudnut speech—a chore that had become increasingly difficult, in large part because Bob kept finding less time to mull what I wrote. I did not welcome these extra demands, but I'll confess that as I finished a new speech on this glowingly brilliant day (the subject was gun control, urging that the "hair trigger" be outlawed in the manufacture of domestic firearms), I was in a state of arousal. It was not uncommon to find myself thus when I worked, and it was easy to trace its origins on this spring day, which had begun as usual. I had strolled through the busy, cluttered newsroom, nodding to friends and others, pleased to see a newcomer beam when I gave a sign of recognition; and, as usual, I'd instinctively speeded up at the sight of Aileen Frugtsaft, with whom I'd had very little to do in the past few years and who had put on weight and seemed ever more angry.

In any event, entering my private office, I had surprised my young blond secretary in the act of adjusting her panty hose and, in the process, had gotten quite a good glimpse of her privates. She blushed charmingly and apologized elaborately (even as I attempted to assure her that apologies were not needed), but while I sat at my desk and composed my column (Israel, the Mets) and then my confidential chore for Bob (hair triggers), that fuzzed dark image stayed with me. In any case, I believe that is why I canceled a lunch with an important State Department source and returned home at midday—with the object, to be blunt, of exercising marital prerogatives that hadn't been exercised in a while.

It is such an old story, isn't it? But even as I heard those distant peeps of pleasure, I didn't absorb them. As I once observed, epigrammatically, there is a moment between experiencing reality and grasping it. Yet those very sounds made me dash to the second floor, where I saw—it *is* such an old story!—Bob Hudnut, who was on his back and therefore the first to see me. The rapid, yet languid rise and fall above him was not interrupted for several seconds, until Alison made a quarter-turn and, with a tiny squeal, sprang upward, as if lighter than air, leaving the object upon which she'd impaled herself standing aloft and alone—an image of the senator I will not forget for as long as I live.

"It's not what you think, Brandon," Bob said at once, quickly putting on a white shirt, a red-and-blue rep tie, and a dark-blue suit. Alison, meanwhile, dashed to the bathroom, her pinkish buttocks aquiver, and then I heard the shower spurting.

"This has never happened before," my old friend went on, his familiar features unhappy and constricted as he adjusted his tie. "You've got to believe that it meant nothing to me—a moment's weakness. I imagine that you're upset—of course you are—not that I blame you! But you mustn't—you absolutely mustn't—let this ruin our friendship or our collaboration." He paused, his voice a little shaky as his thick fingers brushed back his tawny hair. "I know you're far too rational for an episode like this to affect all of that."

I did not, of course, want to sever our ties, and I felt, most of all, sadness as Bob fixed me with a pleading gaze. I wanted to comfort him, to pat his head as I would a wounded animal. Yet I was wounded, too.

"I mean, my God! I'm a man, Brandon!" he went on, as we heard the shower. "You know what that means. You understand a man's weakness." Bob patted the front of his trousers as he zipped them up.

I did know. Powerful men have powerful drives. I recognized that in myself, and several times I'd written sympathetically of Jack Kennedy when his past became public. (I've been less charitable with public men like Clinton at the end of our shameless century.) I wanted to forgive Bob, who seemed genuinely distraught; yet he had, in the fullest sense, betrayed me. To use the vernacular, he had fucked my wife.

"You have to forget this, old pal," Bob said, and grinned, while I thought of Bertrand Russell's axiom that all human activity is prompted by desire.

At that moment, I was not sure what to do, or how to forgive, or whether this episode argued against Bob's fitness for high office. But as Alison returned from the shower, a towel draped across much of her body, goose-bumped and white, but rosy, too, her eyes bashfully cast downward, I knew how difficult it would be for the three of us simply to pick up where we'd left off.

*   *   *

Between Alison and myself, in fact, it was over, and after a few strained weeks, we decided to separate. "To tell you the truth," she said at one point in our discussions, "my feelings for you lie somewhere between indifference and revulsion." After I insisted that she leave my house (I had full title), she began telling her few friends that my feelings toward Hudnut (I no longer thought of him as "Bob") were not entirely natural. I'll never forgive her for that, or for telling others that our physical relationship had been "pathetic."

As for Hudnut, our friendship had lasted more than twenty years, and I suppose that I still saw him as a chum, despite his imperfections. When I met him for dinner a few days later, at a bistro close to Union Station, he appeared momentarily uncomfortable. Then he told me an amusing story about a Missouri hog farmer whose animals had begun to breed too rapidly. "I reckon that sort of thing can happen to the best of friends," he said with a high twang and a withered smile, adding, "I do apologize for letting my dick out of its cage once too often." We laughed together, even though I hadn't faced the implications of Hudnut's flaws, or, for that matter, my own. Neither of us spoke about his political plans.

It was about then that I began to feel less comfortable in crowds. "Go very light on the vices, such as carrying on in society," Satchel Paige said. "The social ramble ain't restful." Paige was very wise, yet to be a journalist in Washington, at least at my level and in my time, makes the Paigean ramble a requirement. It is a rarefied atmosphere, and when I'm with my peers, we seem to know that we cannot part from one another knowing less. But I began to suspect that my peers were looking at me differently and taking me less seriously.

It was therefore a relief to spend time with my daughter, and I always looked forward to our chats, hoping for signs of intellectual maturity. Daphne was, I hope I've made clear, a spirited and intelligent young woman, although unable wholly to escape the vacant obsessions of adolescence: an absorption in boyfriends, shopping, and her appearance. Yet, now and again, she would ask about my work, as if she suddenly grasped that it brought me into contact with the essential people of our century. I particularly remember when Daphne asked if Hudnut, whom she'd known since childhood, could ever be President; and I had shrugged, for I'd seen political hopes dashed in ways that she had not. "You know, Daphne," I said, speaking as much to myself, "the American people have a way of picking the right person. What I do believe is this: If Hudnut is that person, we will pick him."

Daphne, with the blanked-out expression of adolescence, then said something that ought to have made me curious: "I always found him very attractive, even when I was little, even though he's, like, so much older."

"Hudnut is my age," I said. "Exactly my age—old enough to be your father."

"There is something unique about him, though," Daphne said. "He also seems a lot younger than you. Maybe if you lost some weight—no offense, Dad."

"None taken," I replied, but I recalled Alison's frequent complaint that the weight I'd gained in the last few years had affected our lovemaking. Recently, when I'd seen myself on television, I'd noticed that my chin rippled and my jacket could not close.

I thanked God that Daphne seemed to know nothing about Hudnut and Alison, who had swiftly taken herself and her little literary agency to the vicious byways of New York. With the staggering egocentricity of the young, Daphne had not seemed even to notice Alison's removal from my life. Now she almost mumbled when she said, "I might volunteer for his campaign if he decided, you know, to run." As I buzzed my girl to fetch coffee, I told Daphne that Hudnut very likely would run—and would probably say so soon. I believed that Daphne's diffident murmuring, signaling an appetite for politics, was her way of seeking my approval.

It was one of those rare chances to be alone with my daughter, who at one moment was an exceptionally attractive young woman (with a strong resemblance to her mother) and still a playful child. I adored her, and, thinking back, I'm sure that she was attempting to tell me something else. One of my flaws is that I am not always a good listener. My chief flaw is an inability to recognize my other flaws.

It was, in fact, in the spring of 1987, not long after Daphne's sixteenth birthday, that Hudnut declared his presidential ambition. I was there to witness his performance in the Senate Caucus Room, and I, as I had intended to do with Bobby Kennedy in the same venue so many years before, acclaimed it. Hudnut wore a dark-blue suit, a white shirt, and a familiar red-and-blue rep tie, and when I watched him running stubby fingers through thick hair, I was stirred by the thought that he embodied our future, that he could strangely excite the American heart. (At the same time, I had the odd sensation that reality, as I'd come to know it, was being erased.) On that day, Hudnut said, "We have inherited the world, but I fear that we do not understand the responsibility of our inheritance." (We debated changing that to the "burden of our inheritance," for Hudnut was fond of "burden.") On nuclear arms, he said, "The weapons that could incinerate the world could also wipe out the terrible diseases that have plagued mankind." And: "Every American ought to be able to walk in our cities without—

210

let's speak plainly—fear of being kicked in the crotch." He talked about "cooperation with bad countries," and, as the bright lights dazzled and cameramen hurried (I sometimes think that the world is ruled by stocky, bearded men with video apparatuses on their shoulders and battery packs around their waists), he spoke about the burden of race. If I hadn't believed in all of this, I would never have continued to do for him what I, by now a trifle reluctantly, did. Looking back, I suppose I should have known that a final break lay ahead.

Certainly I was troubled by Hudnut's intimacy with my family—that knowing, physical reference to Gretchen and his treachery with Alison—not to speak of his cruelty toward his institutionalized former wife, Gwendolyn. All of this contributed to the *perception* that he was a person capable of doing horrid things. Yet most of the time I thought that I'd come to terms with this side of him; I understood it, for I was guilty of misbehavior, too. More than once, I found myself making love to women whose names I cannot use, who were drawn to me by my fame and influence. (More than once, I stared at the card on which the girl I'd met in Hudnut's apartment, the one with pale-brown skin and pigtails, had written her telephone number and name: Lascala. Each time, I folded it away, quickly quickly.)

After the Alison episode, Hudnut and I undoubtedly felt a personal strain whenever we spoke, elliptically, of my role in a Hudnut administration (I thought of Lippmann at Wilson's side during the Paris Peace Conference, or Schlesinger next to Kennedy). My doubts about him grew even as circumstances, ineluctably, conspired against me; and no doubt

I was affected by the hideous smiles that seemed to quiveringly appear whenever I entered a room filled with people who knew me (on the Paigean ramble). I also felt I was being avoided. Several times I attempted to call Madeleine Whitbridge, only to be told that she, mysteriously, could not come to the phone.

Then—how this hurts!—Aileen Frugtsaft, my onetime intimate friend, started nosing into my collaboration with the nascent Hudnut campaign. (I still become furious when I think of Frugtsaft, her voice a mixture of gloating and commiseration, calling to get a "quote" as if I were a mouse and she the trap.) As I told Miss Frugtsaft forthrightly, I've never pretended to be a workaday journalist; I was not put on this planet simply to take notes. I urged her not to write her little story, but I didn't beg. No one who knew me could doubt my motives, I assured her, and those who doubted me certainly could not know me.

*   *   *

How do I describe the next terrible months? To begin, Aileen's incomprehensible story (in which I was made to say, "I am no mere journalist") nearly ruined me. There followed a curious public glee at my discomfiture, especially from people like Lionel Heftihed, who pounced at once, dredging up columns which, taken out of context, made it appear that I had long fawned over Hudnut. (Lionel had evidently spent years readying this attack, which was plucked from his unanticipated book about journalism in our city; I was flattered by his attention.) Then there were those editors who self-righteously canceled my column and wrote primping columns of their own—sometimes two or three; they seemed incapable of stopping themselves—to explain why they'd done away with mine. I particularly recall a midwestern windbag, one Bradshaw C——, whose condemnation exploded with indignation. I'd "sullied the newspaper trade," he wrote in his Chicago newspaper, and "lowered the barrier." Quite a mouthful, Bradshaw! I thought when C—— (I've decided not to print his full name) was arrested in a Wrigley Park men's room (the Cubs winning four to one), engaged in a consensual act with a homosexual predator. I can't entirely fault NBC for cancel-ing my contract (the facile and too-good-looking Cat Sturdy took my place), but why did my former fellow pan-elists keep chewing it over? Only the *Washington Insights* veteran Chuck Moldine, still articulate, had the decency to say "enough." The vengefulness of my peers made me think of Marlowe's hero, who cries, "But Faustus's offence can ne'er be pardoned; the serpent that tempted Eve may be saved, but not Faustus." And not, I realized, me.

Through it all, I tried to write about the sort of policy questions that have always engaged me (I had recently met Mangosuthu Buthelezi and, in my distraction, misjudged the future of South Africa). I also tried to lunch regularly with my sources, and kept spottily in touch with Hudnut, who, thoughtfully, had autographed a collection of his speeches and sent copies to myself and my daughter, Daphne. My final break with Hudnut, when it came, had causes other than my professional embarrassment, and you may guess what they were. Not that I didn't question my own judgment: Should I have taken more seriously his manly weakness, or the personal peculiarities that I've cata-logued? Should I have noticed something odd in Daphne's fluttery enthusiasm for this old family friend?

* * *

Here I must make another admission: that, distraught over my disintegrating career, I nearly had a single, brief, meaningless encounter with Lascala, the young African-American whose card I'd found in an unswept pocket. I knew that it would have been wrong; when I dialed her number, I'd hoped she wouldn't answer, and when she showed up at my front door, I wished for the strength not to let her in. But Lascala was older than her years; as Swift wrote, we human brutes "are lured by their appetites to their destruction," and one cannot always resist the delicate caress, the enchantment of peachlike breasts. When Lascala stretched and yawned and looked at me in a way that made her eyes seem unnaturally large, I began to tremble and perspire; I felt a curious weightlessness, as if I'd become a witness to the behavior of some other reckless creature; and I felt a powerful urge to intervene. To my relief, I heard my own voice, as if from a distance, instructing her to leave, and then, all at once, she said, "Mister, do you got a daughter named Daphne?" My surprise was such that my heart thumped noisily and my perspiration chilled. "I feel pretty sure it's her," she said, taking my hot hand with her cool, slender fingers, and went on, "Just between us, you might want to check in on that senator friend of yours." I nodded, quite speechless. I cannot describe what I felt; I can only say that I was in such shock that Lascala had to ask me twice to give her quite a large sum of money, and that I felt inexpressibly sad when she told me that once, in our very brief conversation, I'd called her by another name. "You a nice man," she said, charitably, and asked, "Who Zoe?"

I suppose I must go into some detail on what happened next—what I saw when I decided to poke my uninvited head into Hudnut's apartment. I had driven rapidly, unhappily, to his Southeast block and the pastel-colored row house whose basement he rented, and for a minute or so I simply stood outside, pacing. Half a block away, two or three young men leaned against a dented automobile, laughing at something, and I envied them their world far from mine; I smiled at them, but my goodwill was not returned. Then I stepped down toward the basement entrance, rang a bell, and, when a girlish inquisitor asked who was there, declared in my falsetto disguise, "It's me!" As the door buzzed open, I walked into Hudnut's darkened, dusty flat (tan shades were drawn over the barred windows, hiding the bright light of early afternoon) and saw two or three of his minority students lying on the floor of the living room, propped up by pillows, watching the drama of a television game show unfold; they wore blue jeans and T-shirts emblazoned with the portraits of musicians. The floor was filthy—aged popcorn and nacho chips were embedded in a dark-red square of carpet—and copies of the *Congressional Record* were scattered about, many of their pages ripped. When, in the dimness, I went to the entrance of what evidently was the bedroom, someone, with a squealing titter, said, "I wouldn't go there, mister," but by then it was too late.

When I opened the door to that room, I spotted Hudnut himself, disrobed apart from a golden breastplate that covered his freckled shoulders and hairy chest. In front of him, bending over a queen-size bed, was Daphne, my daughter, who ought to have been in school. Her hands were tied together by leather thongs, her dear, young breasts drooping, as Hudnut maneuvered from behind, satisfying his urges as his thick peasant fingers gripped her delicate hips. I felt an absolute jolt—no other word suffices—of astonishment, and as this scene progressed for a few more seconds with harmonic moans (the thrusts ever more rapid, ever closer to release—phrases I never dreamed I could pen), I thought that if someone handed me a pistol, I would have murdered Hudnut at that instant. In fact, I said, "I can't imagine an explanation for this," or something to that effect.

"I can't explain it, either, Brandon," Hudnut replied, after a moment or so of extraordinary silence, ended by applause from the bright television screen in the adjoining room. Then Hudnut hurriedly dropped his breastplate with a clang and rapidly slipped into his dark-blue suit, his white shirt, a handsome Italian silk tie, a neatly folded handkerchief, and the rest, as Daphne appeared slowly to crumple, whimpering, to the floor and the other girls, who had come to the door, looked on. "But I'm mortified," he added.

"It's a sign of a total lack of control," I said, my anger dampened by my state of shock.

"Brandon, I'm just a man," Hudnut said as he had before, a crooked grin springing out, with accompanying creases, a wink topping it off. "I've told you that." He pointed to his fly and added, in black dialect, "Mista John-son, he be horny." Hudnut then headed very rapidly into the living room, and, without looking back at any of us, opened the door and raced up to the street.

Feeling helpless, I extended my arms to my second-born, but Daphne began to stare up from her crouched position as if I were an enemy. How I wish I could have done so many things over. How I loved her! "Oh, Daddy, come off it," she said, getting up almost languidly, lifting her arms, as if flaunting her shameless costume. "Like I didn't *tell* you how Bobby turned me on?" *Bobby!* she'd said. "Like this is some kind of sur*prise*—for the guy joined at Bobby's hip?"

I shook my head, which had become so light that I felt either it would float away or I would pass out.

"I mean, give me a fucking break," Daphne said, and all at once she shimmied as if to further flaunt her lewd state.

"Come with me," I said, but she just stayed there, sway-ing, then rotating, with a fixed smile and a single, almost imperceptible sniffle. "Please," I begged, while the rest of them stared at me and kept staring until I managed some-how to leave, wobbling back, upward, onto the street, where the sun scalded my eyes. From the corner, I could see the Capitol dome, so I knew where I was, but I felt, for the first time in my life, lost.

                              *   *   *

There, it's done; I've set down the full squalidness of it; and for a day or so I held to the illusion that it was a private matter, forgetting that gossip has an adhesive quality—it clings to one. I had tried again, without success, to reach Madeleine Whitbridge, but everyone else in Washington seemed to know that something had happened between Hudnut and my daughter. I got my first intimation of this when I ran into Beano at a cocktail party down the street from my Volta Place home. Just as I'd swallowed a hot, stuffed mushroom that burnt the back of my throat and made a molten path to my stomach, he shook his head and said, "It's been a rough couple of weeks, huh?"

"The fucking worst," I replied, knowing that his sympathy was not entirely genuine; he'd undoubtedly approved Aileen Frugtsaft's story about me. "Fucking awful," I added.

If there were times when I didn't think about my near ruin—my newspaper clients had shrunk almost overnight from four hundred to a few dozen and my syndicate was thinking of dropping me—more often I could think of little else. Then Beano said, "Listen, what do you hear about the Von Helsings?" Before I could reply to this mystifying query about the newspaper's owners, Beano edged away and into an amusing conversation with a German banker. Other guests looked toward me, then averted their eyes; I suspected them, and everyone, of knowing my secrets and thinking less of me.

I tried several times to call Daphne, but she wouldn't discuss what had happened. Gretchen, however, would, and she appeared far angrier than was fair to me. I got a sample of her disapproval when she visited my office unannounced—her first visit ever to this lair—as I was polishing a tough column on the Bundesbank. Gretchen looked so beautiful that my happy impulse was to smile, but she took no pleasure in seeing me. When I kissed her cheek, she recoiled.

"You chubby, self-satisfied twit," Gretchen said, her voice rising so that I hurried to shut my office door. "Daphne was victimized by a sick, ambitious man that you brought into our house. You condoned it—you probably encouraged it."

"She told you?" I whispered.

"She was hysterical! She could hardly *speak!* Do you have any *idea* what she's been through?"

I looked at Gretchen's contorted face and swore to her

that I'd had no idea what was going on until I saw the two of them in congress (the pun was not intentional). Yet her stream of words made me wonder if perhaps, in some intuitive way, I *had* known precisely what was going on. But, no, that was ridiculous; and, furthermore, Gretchen had no idea of the pain she was causing me at that moment. I lashed out.

"You cannot deny," I said, "that you granted your own intimate favors to this sick, ambitious man, as you call him. I have to tell you, Gretchen, that he's praised your sexual talents, your excellent pussy—he's a big fan of yours." I was ashamed at having struck this low blow until Gretchen murmured, "After you, Brandon, I needed it."

At that point in our talk, Gretchen went on to say something about my "smug expression" (rather, I had been deeply insulted), and attempted to punch my face. I managed to block her right arm with my left wrist, but in a surprise move, she smacked me hard with her left palm, leaving a small bruise along a cheek, and ripped off my bow tie. I felt something collapse within me and, to my surprise, found myself close to tears. It was the strangest sensation, especially when those tears burst out of me, uncontrolled; it left me depleted. It was as if I'd suddenly gotten a glimpse of something I'd greatly desired; and then—before I quite knew what that something was—it was taken away.

"My God, Brandon, what is it?" Gretchen said, as if she cared. She had never seen me like this, and through my wet eyes, I noticed that she wasn't looking at me—rather that her gaze was fixed elsewhere in my office. I bowed my head, still making inarticulate sounds as she left, hurriedly, ending our colloquy. But I silently repeated her question: What was it indeed? I had no idea. As I'd wept, I had thought, in a blurred way, about so many things: about Daphne, of course, and of her distress, but also, inevitably, about my life, and of how it had come to this. A moment later, when I looked up, I saw to my horror that the picture of my long-ago self with Jack Kennedy—tie clasp and all—was gone.

As for Hudnut, he waited a day or so to call, and when he did, it was a brief, awkward conversation. He said he'd totally forgotten that Daphne was my daughter, that he was very bad with names and faces—after all, he met so many people in the course of a day. I didn't find him persuasive. Hudnut then reminded me of our friendship, which I said was now canceled. I told him that I planned to use my column to respond to Aileen Frugtsaft's little story, and would fully confess my role in his public life. But, I went on, I was going to allude to his shameless personal life as well. I quoted the wise Dryden—"Better shun the bait than struggle in the snare"—which puzzled him. When I said that I planned to call him "a clever and talented man, but not someone worthy of a nation's trust—or a friend's," he abruptly hung up. We haven't spoken since.

Several weeks later, I was called to the newsroom to hear the announcement, delivered by the newspaper's red-faced and white-haired publisher, that the Von Helsings had decided to sell the *Telegram* to one of the chains. Many of us in the circling crowd gasped; I saw that Aileen Frugtsaft began to cry, and I almost pitied her until she hugged another reporter a little too firmly. I was stunned, and as I watched the moths fly about the flickering poles of fluorescent light, I expected worse news to come.

It did not, of course, take long for the new owners to discover that the separate parts of their new acquisition—downtown real estate, a radio station in northern Virginia, part of a cable system in some dismal New England town—were worth far more than an ancient newspaper with its tiny profit, and within a few weeks, they posted a notice that the *Telegram* itself was going out of business.

During the last few days of publication, I was surprised at how sentimental I had become. Everything that I'd known for more than twenty years—the disintegrating envelopes stuffed with clippings; metal desks with coffee rings; keyless typewriters, trays, and wobbly chairs; crumpled bags of forgotten vending machine food; dead mice and moth skin; nameplates and rotary telephones—was tossed out, along with me. (My sentiment extended to my old colleague, Jervis Tramm, now almost sixty, who asked me for a job reference that I could not, in good conscience, give him.) As the presses cranked out the final edition (which was briefly collected by those who prize trophies of finality), most of us went to watch. It is the sort of change that reminds us of our fragility; we're much like clocks, after all, although without a wind-up mechanism.

*   *   *

Over the next few years, with the newspaper gone and my column no longer visible in Washington, a peculiar thing happened: People who ought to have known better thought that I'd retired, and for a time (in the early nineties), it was as if I did not quite exist. The truth is that I felt defeated by this turn; it was as if I'd become a pudgy, middle-aged man without a voice. But, as Emerson put it, "a man should learn to detect and watch that gleam of light which flashes across his mind from within," and soon enough, it occurred to me that I was confronting not only my own disappearance, but the diminishment of the printed word. That thought, oddly enough, cheered me, for at the same time I sensed that something encouraging was happening as the century concluded: a seemingly infinite stock of intelligent ideas was being dispensed at all times by television's fresh new channels. I was wanted again. Soon enough, I found myself appearing on more cable programs than any single person could manage to watch.

I'm wanted, or so they tell me, because I offer a rare kind of depth. As George Bush the elder said, when he encouraged me to take this autobiographical leap, I've "been there"—I've been privileged to know, and sometimes befriend, the most vital people of our time. I've rubbed shoulders (literally so; the phrase resonates for me) with everyone, and we've met at receptions, dinner parties, foreign capitals, television studios, and funerals—a great waltz across history's stage. There have been so many handshakes (firm and limp), whispered confidences, back-pats, arm grips, and encounters at the urinal that it becomes a little hazy, and that, I suppose, is why I've not thought it necessary to set down my impressions of every American big shot, not to mention Helmut Kohl (or was it Helmut Schmidt?) and Margaret Thatcher and all those French and Italian and Japanese people and Lech Walesa, the heroic Pole, whose translator so let me down that I never had any idea what the little man was talking about.

Nor, for that matter, do I plan to say more about Hudnut, although now and then I spot him walking about town and it is possible that he spots me. I will never forgive him, of course, but, with a shudder of commiseration, I did send him a note on the occasion of his cheerless memoir, *Their Bodies, Myself*. And, although we still do not speak, now and then we appear together on television; with his enduring thick hair and gaunt face, Hudnut, too, remains in demand. After all, he is running once more for President and his poll numbers are very high.

People who send me letters from the heartland tell me that I'm still good at this—still witty and articulate and informed; sometimes, though, I feel as if I'm everywhere at once, talking into camera after camera about the world of today and yesterday, unblinking, my eyebrows perpetually raised. Sometimes I fear that I've gotten lost in a swarm of disembodied gestures, and that no one really listens to, or remembers, a single word I say.

I tend to have such cheerless thoughts at funerals, as on the recent autumn morning that I said farewell to Madeleine Whitbridge, who had died (quietly, as one says) in her sleep. I had been following the World Series, that autumnal ballet, when I came across Madeleine's short obituary. I regretted not knowing that she'd been in a lengthy coma, which explained why she'd not returned my calls. I wondered who would be at the service (at an Episcopal church convenient to my house) and had the disturbing thought that there would be no one with whom I could discuss the mourners in an intelligent fashion other than Madeleine herself. I fought off the curious urge to telephone her.

On the morning of the ceremony, I walked the short distance alone, thinking that the streets of Georgetown had become shabbier and that I'd become shorter of breath. It was a day of rain alternating with flashes of sun; outside the church, where the brick sidewalk was covered with shiny, colored leaves, I saw only a few people I knew, among them Aileen Frugtsaft, whom I'd not seen since the *Telegram* closed and she'd moved to the Eastern Shore to write about gardening. I'd not been able to speak civilly to Frugtsaft after her ruinous little scoop, but I believe that her eyes attempted to find mine as we passed down the darkened aisle, or perhaps my vision was fooled by the sharply lighted out-of-doors. I thought that she'd put on considerable weight, but in the few polite words we eventually exchanged, she assured me that she was happy. Despite everything, I was glad to hear it.

Close by, I saw Beano and his angular wife, Samantha, who did not take note of my friendly nod, and behind them was Gretchen, whose eyes were red from crying (perhaps because her own parents had gotten send-offs within the same church), and who clutched her husband's arm. Even these many years after her Nora-like decision, I could remember her darkling thighs and womanly softness and smiled to myself, though I was still furious at her brazen theft. Lionel looked frail, but so did several other acquaintances whose names I could not quite recall. As more people filed in, I stood and stretched and looked all about, to see who else might be there and made out many sharp, unformed faces, such as the slow-witted and good-looking Cat Sturdy, my replacement on NBC, who was utterly out of place. When I glanced again in Beano's direction (still, he did not seem to see me), I saw in front of him a woman with thick dark hair, wearing a wide-brimmed black hat, and it was not until she smiled that I recognized those full lips as belonging to Esther Goldenstein. Perhaps she found me unrecognizable (the last time I'd seen her, I was still married to Alison), although many people have said that, apart from the weight

I've put on and my gray, thinning hair and lengthening crow's-feet, I never seemed to age.

The organist played Bach (I believe it was "Herz und Mund und Tat und Leben") as people kept making their way in, tripping over one another in the pews, exchanging shrugs of apology and sorrow, until the small church was almost filled. The minister, who had known Madeleine and also her husband, Willy, spoke first and praised her kindness and friendship; so did Jasper Munroe, who had to be helped to the pulpit and was unable to finish his remarks. The third speaker was a fierce-looking woman in a black-and-turquoise dress—Madeleine's daughter, Ariadne, whom most of us had never met, and who said, inexplicably and rudely, "The best thing I ever did was to move away from this rotten city, and the worst thing my mother did was to stay here," patting her dry eyes.

No one had asked me to speak, and I was not listed on the program, but I thought that I should say something anyway, and, before the next hymn could begin, I made my way to the front, stumbling once, feeling slightly winded. "Once I was young," I told the mourners, surprised at not hearing an appreciative chuckle. Then I took a deep breath and went on. "When I first came to Washington, Madeleine took a shine to me and taught me valuable lessons; and when I was older, she stuck by me and gave me advice and information. I was lucky to be her friend and her confidant, and I hope that she was lucky to be mine." My remarks silenced the crowd utterly.

After the final hymn (the words, "For those in peril on the sea," also honored Willy Whitbridge, who had perished

on water), and when all of us had filed out into the bright-
ness of the day, I had the very odd sense that I'd become
part of an awkward, incomplete tableau. Many of us stood
about, not knowing quite when to go, or where, and I
looked around, waiting for someone to greet me. When I
found Esther and went to her side, she let me kiss her powdered cheek, tickling me with her hair. I discovered that I
was weeping, a habit I seem to have picked up in later years.

"Brandon, you're still a silly rabbit," she whispered with
affection, leaning closer (I saw gray strands), her breath a
little hot. "I hope you know that I've kept up with your
frightful problems. I almost called—you poor thing. But
then I put it off, and it got too late." She shook her head
and said, "What are you doing now?"

I tried to tell her that my life was full—the column,
while not widely read anymore, kept me busy; and, of
course, my cable appearances, especially at times of national
mourning. When I asked her about herself, Esther said that
she was still a book editor, and named several of her writers—people she evidently regarded as important. Then I
had to turn away from her increasingly mournful eyes.

I heard myself say, "You were my good friend, but I
never appreciated it. I remember how you looked after me
when I first came to town. I suppose I was sometimes heed-
less." She squeezed my hand. For some reason, I thought of
the sheer white blouse that she used to wear, and how I'd
hurt her feelings more than once. Onlookers no doubt
thought I was grieving, but in fact it was this other, newer
sensation: that I'd lost something of immense value, but,
with the illogic of a dream, had no idea what it was.

* * *

Eventually, most of the crowd, including Esther and Beano and Gretchen and Aileen, bunched into smaller groups, such as the fawning little circle around Cat Sturdy, and climbed into waiting limousines and went their way, but without me. I didn't mind, although I was surprised that Esther did not want to talk longer and catch up; and I was unaccountably happy that she put her head out the window as her black car pulled away, and that she waved to me when it turned and headed out of sight. By now, though, my thoughts were elsewhere, on my work and on life itself. I wondered what I might say in my next column, but also on television that weekend, when I was booked for quite a few programs.

I knew, certainly, that I would talk about Madeleine (she would also be the subject of my next column), and I would say how fortunate I was to have known someone like her. I would suggest that she shared my worries about the cynicism that has suffused American life, and that she would be baffled by the foolish moralizing and terrifying ambition that encloses us. Madeleine, I would add, understood the obligation I feel to young people, and why I become discouraged whenever I visit college campuses (although I've always found it hard to take seriously anyone younger than myself): Does anyone want to hear my thoughts on the Kennedy legacy? I'll ask. How about Vietnam? Watergate, anyone? The decline of liberalism from Roosevelt to Clinton? Race, poverty, education, pollution, crime, cinematic violence? None of that, they say with their silence; they would rather speculate about Hudnut's appetites, my putative agenda, my estrangements, and for that I blame people like Lionel, whose shoddy book about journalism will forever embarrass the critics who praised it and the Pulitzer board that dishonored itself.

I prefer to speak to an imagined audience made up of people I wish I'd seen more of, such as my children (Branny's face, scarily, has become my young face, although his blond, wavy hair is painted a bright red and cigarettes dangle from his pimpled lips); and my father, whom I visited at Millard Fillmore Hospital hours before he slipped into a coma—he let loose a strange, shrill cackle when I confided my plan to write a memoir; and those with whom I had regrettable misunderstandings, worthy comrades like Tobias Goldenstein and Chet Budge and our little band of editorial writers. It's easy to become melancholy—as Longfellow put it, "The leaves of memory seem to make a mournful rustling in the dark"—but more often I reflect, happily, on my modest successes and ephemeral pleasures. See, there they were; and, like words on paper, there was I.

ACKNOWLEDGMENTS

* * *

I would never have begun this project without an extra push from my literary agent, Alison Macciola. I become uncomfortable when I think, although I rarely do, about her former role as my wife, but I never doubted her perspicacity or professionalism. Alison reminded me that I've had a rare vantage point and ought to have the last word.

Special thanks—and apologies—begin with my daughter. When Daphne agreed to speak to me, certain subjects were off-limits: her unorthodox profession as a private model, her whereabouts, and Hudnut. I had intended to respect all of these wishes and hope, therefore, that she'll forgive me for revealing some of what she called, in her colorful way, "all that painful shit," and will come to understand that truth may be a heartless tyrant. Thanks also to

Branny, who is bravely "getting straight" and shared some of his recovered memories. (Wing, too.)

I'm grateful to several careful readers of the manuscript: Morton Manatie, who remembered some amusing times in the early days of *Washington Insights*; Jasper Munroe (whose long-term memory is not impaired); Deputy Secretary X, who refused to see me but agreed to confirm some important facts; and Gwendolyn Hudnut, who taught me the real meaning of the words "to heal" and "to unload." Any errors that crept in may well be mine.

I owe a special debt to my editor, Esther Goldenstein. I had always imagined that she would choose a livelihood more satisfying than her work as a receptionist (albeit a receptionist with ripening editorial talent), but never dreamed that she would flourish so; her fine blue pencil guided nearly every word and comma. Although we've not seen one another for many years (that was "the deal," as she put it, when she took on my book: that I'd stay away from her), she knows that I remain eager to cross the moat of distance and to defeat the assault of time.

INDEX

* * *

ABOUT THE AUTHOR

JEFFREY FRANK is a senior editor at
The New Yorker, and was formerly an
editor and writer at *The Washington
Post* and *The Washington Star*. He lives
in Manhattan with his wife, Diana.